The officer ran toward the coach. Justin fired again. He missed his mark. The man was on top of him in a moment. Justin scrambled to his feet. He tried to fend off the saber stroke with his musket. The force of the blow knocked the weapon from his hands. By the time Theo reached him, the officer had brought up his blade again. Had Theo not pulled Justin aside, the saber would have struck him in the throat. Instead, it laid open the lad's forehead and cheek. The man braced to make another attack.

"Kill him!" Justin turned his bloody face to Theo, violet eyes blazing. "Kill him!"

LLOYD ALEXANDER, a resident of Drexel Hill, Pennsylvania, is the author of The Prydain Chronicles, including *The Book of Three, The High King, Taran Wanderer, The Black Cauldron,* and *The Castle of Llyr.*

WESTMARK

Lloyd Alexander

For those who regret their many imperfections, but know it would be worse having none at all.

Published by
Bantam Doubleday Dell Books for Young Readers
a division of
Bantam Doubleday Dell Publishing Group, Inc.
1540 Broadway
New York, New York 10036

The trademark Laurel-Leaf Library® is registered in the U.S. Patent and Trademark Office.

The trademark Dell® is registered in the U.S. Patent and Trademark Office.

ISBN: 0-440-99731-3

RL: 6.0

Reprinted by arrangement with Dutton Children's Books, a division of Penguin Books USA Inc.

Printed in the United States of America

June 1982

20 19 18

RAD

CONTENTS

PART ONE
The Printer's Devil

❧

1

Theo, by occupation, was a devil. That is, he worked as apprentice and general servant to Anton, the printer. Before that, he was lucky enough to be an orphan, for the town fathers of Dorning prided themselves in looking after their needy. So, instead of sending him away to a King's Charity House, where he would be made miserable, they arranged the same for him locally. He was farmed out first to a cooper, then to a saddler, and in both cases did badly. Accidentally, he had learned to read, which in some opinion spoiled him for anything sensible. Anton finally agreed to take in the boy and teach him his trade.

Theo proved good at this work, and he and his master dealt very well with each other. Anton never whipped his devil, and Theo never gave him cause. Once thickset and muscular, Anton had begun sagging a little around the middle. His passion was his press, and he was forever fussing with it. Since he kept all the smudges for himself and his clothing, his pages came out spotless. He was, in fact, a fine craftsman. Scholars from the university at Freyborg had brought him treatises to print. The business dried up after the king appointed Cabbarus chief minister. By order of Cabbarus, official approval was required for every publication; even a text on botany was eyed with suspicion. Anton was reduced to turning out visiting cards for the gentry and billheads for the tradespeople. He was no worse off than other printers in Westmark. A number had been arrested, and some of them hanged. So, to that extent, he was considerably better off.

As for Theo, he loved virtue, despised injustice, and was always slightly hungry. Apart from that, he was reasonably happy.

One day in early spring, Anton went out on business, leaving his devil in charge. Theo cleaned and sorted letter blocks, finished his other chores by the end of the afternoon, and was ready to close shop when a dwarf came strutting in like a gamecock.

A riding coat swept to the little man's boot heels, an enormous cocked hat perched on the side of his head. He stood, hat included, no higher than the middle button of Theo's jacket. In swagger, he took up more room than half a dozen taller men.

Theo was glad to see any size of customer, but before he could wish him good-day or ask his business, the stranger went peering into the ink pots, rattling the wooden cases, fingering the stacks of paper, and squinting sidelong at the press.

At last he stopped, hooked his thumbs into his waistcoat, and declared, in a voice half bullfrog, half bass drum, "Musket!"

Theo, bemused, could only stare. The dwarf snapped his fingers.

"Musket! That's my name."

The dwarf shook his head impatiently, as if Theo should have known without being told, then waved a hand around the shop.

"You're the only printer, I suppose, in Upper Dismal or whatever you call this place?"

"Sir," began Theo, "to tell you the truth—"

"Don't."

"What I mean is I'm not the printer. I'm only his devil."

"You're a big one, then. I'll say that much for you," replied Musket. "You'll do. You'll have to."

The dwarf whipped off his hat, loosing a burst of ginger-colored hair, reached into it, and pulled out a number of closely written scraps of paper. He tossed them on the counter.

The pages, from what Theo glimpsed, were the draft for some sort of tract or pamphlet.

"To be printed up. And nicely. No cheap-jack work. It's for Dr. Absalom. He's world-famous. You've heard of him."

Theo admitted he had not, adding that he had never been out of Dorning.

The dwarf gave him a look of pity. "A grown lad like you? And never away from this hole-and-corner? You aren't much in the swim of things, are you?"

Musket now turned his attention to the pamphlet. Tapping his thumb against his fingers, he began rattling off the number of copies, the size, the quality of paper the world-renowned Dr. Absalom insisted on.

The little man was talking about more work than the shop had seen in a year. Theo began calculating in his head how much it would all come to. Musket spared him the trouble by offering his own price, a handsome one, better than handsome. Theo's heart sank at what he heard next.

"Needed tomorrow," said Musket. "First thing."

"Tomorrow? We can't. There's not enough time."

"Take it or leave it. Tomorrow or not at all." The dwarf rocked back and forth on his heels.

Theo's mind raced. He could not bring himself to

turn down such a piece of business. With a master craftsman like Anton, the two of them working all night at top speed, it was possible, though barely so. But the decision was Anton's to make. Theo had never promised work on his own.

"What's it to be, then?" demanded Musket.

"You'll have it. By noon."

The dwarf shot a finger at him. "Nine."

Theo choked a little. "By nine."

"Done!" Musket clapped on his hat and made for the door. "I'll be here to fetch them."

Theo had not a moment to waste. Anton would be overjoyed—or furious at him for making promises he could not keep. From the first days of his apprenticeship, Anton had taught him that his word, once given, must be counted on. As soon as Musket had gone, Theo began studying the scraps of paper to see how best he could arrange his work.

Dr. Absalom, he read, boasted powers of magnetism, hypnotism, and the secret of eternal youth. He also offered to cure, at a modest fee, warts, gout, gallstones, boils, and every other ailment afflicting humankind.

It was rubbish, written surely by Dr. Absalom since only an author could have such a good opinion of himself. Theo had read every book in his master's storeroom: law, science, natural philosophy. Unschooled, he was awed by the learned professors at Freyborg. He could imagine what they would say of the self-styled doctor. Nevertheless, the dwarf had come bursting in like a wind from a world beyond anything Theo knew. He was fascinated in spite of himself and half-believing. His common sense nagged at him. He ignored it.

When Anton came back it was past nightfall. Theo was still at the type case. He had stopped only to light candles. His hand darted over the maze of wooden pi-

geonholes, snatching up letter after letter and dropping the pieces of type into the composing stick in his
other palm. The scrape of Anton's boots on the plank
flooring startled him. He left off and hurried to greet
the printer, who was wearily shedding his coat.

Anton's face, usually cheerful, was gray and
pouchy. Theo, full of his good news, decided that
keeping it for dessert would make it all the better, and
offered to heat a pot of lentils for his master.

"No, no thank you, lad. I lost my appetite at the
notary's. I stopped to remind him of the small matter
of his unpaid account. He let me cool my heels while
he ate a hot supper. Then he swore if I troubled him
again he'd have the law on me."

"He can't. The law's on your side. It says so in Wel-
lek's *Legal Commentaries*. You know that. You printed
it yourself."

"That was before Cabbarus. Books are one thing;
how the world goes now is another."

"King Augustine must have been out of his wits,"
retorted Theo, "taking Cabbarus for any kind of minister, let alone the highest in the kingdom."

"Out of his wits? Yes, with heartbreak, losing the
princess and not another child since then. And that's
six years gone. Queen Caroline faced up to it better
than he did. More's the pity, he could have been a
good king."

"I can understand it broke his heart. The one to
blame is Cabbarus," said Theo. "He's the one who
speaks for the king. No, he does worse than speak. He
lays down the law, if you can call it that, for there's no
justice in it. He has every printer in Westmark by the
throat. Well, I wish I had him by the throat. I wish
somebody would—"

"Enough," said Anton. "I don't want to hear that
sort of talk. I taught you better than that. Oh, I'll
stand up for what's right. And heaven help whoever

lays a finger on my press, for he'll have me to deal with. But neither you, nor I, nor anyone can judge whether a man's fit to live or die."

Theo grinned at him. "That's from *De Rerum Justitiae*. I've been reading it."

Anton chuckled. "Well then, you know as much as I do. Is that how you spend your time when I'm out of the shop? I suppose you could do worse. What are you up to now? I saw you pegging away, but there's no work on hand."

Theo could no longer hold back his news. "There is. It might even be too much."

He quickly told Anton what had happened. Instead of reproaching him, Anton brightened instantly. When he saw how far Theo had already gone with the task, he clapped him on the back and seized an inkstained apron.

"Good lad! I couldn't have managed it better. We may break our backs, but we'll finish in time to suit this fellow Muskrat or whatever he calls himself."

He bustled around the shop, putting out iron frames, blocks, and wedges so as to have all at hand. Theo hurried back to his typesetting and soon lost track of the hours, not even hearing the town clock. Anton, flushed and inky, readied the press. Well before dawn, they began drawing proofs of the first pages.

Theo had picked up a sheet of paper when a battering at the door startled him. He thought, first, that Musket had come for his work sooner than promised; but the pounding was more violent than the dwarf, with all his impatience, could have produced.

He ran to the front of the shop. As he did, the door splintered, burst from its hinges, and crashed inward. Two men in uniform shouldered past him.

2

They were field militia. He recognized the green tunics and white crossbelts. Without thinking, he flung up his arms to defend himself. One of the soldiers, at this movement, swung the butt of his musket and drove it into Theo's ribs. The blow doubled him up. He fell to his knees, clutching his belly, gagging at the pain. The man who struck him glanced down briefly: without malice, without curiosity, as if he found Theo an uninteresting specimen of livestock.

A third figure had stepped into the shop. Cleanshaven, cloaked in dark gray, he wore a tall hat with a curved brim. He could have passed for a merchant or councillor.

The militiamen stiffened to attention.

Anton was shouting and brandishing his inkdauber. The officer paid no heed. He halted in the middle of the shop. In a voice saturated with boredom, having made the same declaration so often that he knew it by rote, he informed Anton that all printing establishments were now, by Royal Warrant, subject to inspection.

"With the view," he went on, "to discover unlawful publications and criminal conduct—"

When it dawned on Anton what the officer was reciting, he burst out laughing. "Unlawful? Criminal? I'll tell you what's criminal here. Lack of business!"

The printer was red-faced and sweating. The officer looked him up and down with distaste, then strode to the worktable. He picked up one of the sheets and scanned it.

"Who is this Absalom? He's a fraud on the very face of it, and who knows what more underneath. We'll have a closer look at him. And you, too." He folded the page and slipped it under his cloak. "Is this the sort of trade you favor?"

"If I only did what suited me I'd starve to death," retorted Anton. "I'm a printer, not a judge."

"Quite so," said the officer. "In which case, show me the license for this publication, and whatever else you've been doing."

Anton glanced at Theo, who just now had struggled to his feet. "Ah—as for that—"

"We'll have it this morning," Theo broke in, "as soon as the town clerk opens his office."

The officer raised his eyebrows. "Will you, indeed? You admit, however, that in fact you have none at present."

"The customer came late in the day," said Theo. "The office was closed. He needed his work done. There was no other way—"

"Except," said the officer, "to break the law. Very well. The case is clear enough."

He nodded curtly to the soldiers and made a gesture toward the press. "Take it down."

"No!" cried Theo. "That's not right! We're not criminals—"

Anton stared in disbelief. The militiamen slung

their muskets and took hold of the press, straining to
topple it. The printer's hesitation lasted barely a moment. As the two laid hands on his press, Anton threw
himself on them. He thrust his dauber into the face of
the closer militiaman. The soldier, under the force of
the blow, pitched into a corner, stunned. Anton
dropped his makeshift weapon and grappled the
man's comrade by the crossbelt.

The soldier broke free. Theo ran to help his master.
From the tail of his eye, he saw the officer reach under his cloak and bring out a pistol, aiming at the rag-
ing printer.

One of the iron frames lay on the worktable. Theo
seized it and swung it upward. The iron twisted in his
grasp, flew slantwise, and struck the officer on the
side of the head. The man grunted and went down.
The pistol discharged into the floor.

The soldier in the corner sat up, trying to rub the
ink from his eyes. His comrade hastily pointed his musket at Theo and fired. The shot went wide; the bullet
splintered one of the type cases.

Theo scarcely heard either explosion. He could not
turn away from the officer sprawled on the floor. The
man's hat had rolled under the table. His face had
gone slack, mouth open; he was bleeding from the
nose, the trickle making a crimson spider web across
his cheek.

The militiaman fumbled his reloading and cursed.
Theo stood rooted. Anton was bawling at him; the
words reached his ears from a distance. He understood none of them.

Next thing he knew, Anton was shoving him out the
door. He found himself running over the cobbles, legs
pumping mechanically. The printer pushed him along
whenever he faltered. They plunged into the shadows
of an alley.

Theo was asking over and over if the man was dead. Anton did not answer, laboring for breath. They ran on, turning from one street into the next. Anton halted and put out a hand to steady himself against the side of a building.

"Out of wind," he gasped. "You—get clear of this." He made a movement with his head. "That way. I'll take the other street. We've a better chance if we separate."

Theo's mind was still in the printshop. It took him a few moments to grasp what his master was telling him. The clatter of boots grew louder behind them.

"Get out!" Anton took Theo by the collar, spun him around, and sent him stumbling across the alley in the opposite direction.

By the time Theo turned back, the printer had vanished. Theo lurched after him, then stopped, uncertain which street Anton had taken. There was a flash, the crack of a shot. He ran blindly ahead.

He had lived all his life in Dorning, but the town had suddenly changed. He recognized nothing. Houses loomed that he had never seen before. He tried to sight the clock tower. He followed one street that appeared familiar. It ended in a blind alley which should not have been there. He doubled back in panic.

The marketplace opened in front of him. How he had reached it, he had no idea; but he knew at least where he was. The Crown Inn was on his left, at the near side of the square. He ran toward it, thinking vaguely that he might hide in the stables. The innyard gates were bolted at this hour. He glanced behind him and saw no one. He leaped up, gained a handhold, and swung himself over.

The windows of the inn were dark. Theo raced across the yard into one of the sheds. A lantern hung on the wall, but there was no sign of Bodo, the stableman. He could not guess whether the fellow was snoring away somewhere or likely to appear at any moment.

Theo had no plan except to rejoin Anton as soon as he collected his wits and his heart stopped pounding. A high-wheeled coach stood at the back of the shed. He saw no better hiding place, went to it, and turned the door handle. It was unlocked. He flung it open and clambered in.

Before he could pull the door shut, a figure popped up like a jack-in-the-box. A cannonball hurtled into his middle and jolted him against the seat.

The cannonball was a head attached to a body that seemed to own more than the usual number of arms and legs, all of which were pummeling him at the same time. An instant later he found himself nose to nose with and staring into the indignant face of the dwarf.

3

"The devil!" cried Musket, in exasperation more than recognition. His eyes, pink with sleep, batted furiously. Shirt unbuttoned, neckerchief askew, he showed nothing of his afternoon jauntiness. "I thought you were a burglar. What are you doing in my coach?"

"They tried to smash our press," blurted Theo, too caught up in his own distress to be surprised at the sight of his onetime customer. "They were going to arrest us."

"You're in trouble with the law?" Musket squinted at him. "Well, don't put us in the same pickle, whatever it is. Out! Off with you!"

"Please—let me rest. I don't know what to do. My master's out there somewhere. They're after him. They'll be after Dr. Absalom, too."

The dwarf had been making every effort to push Theo out of the coach. Hearing this, he stopped abruptly.

"Sit there," ordered Musket. "Don't leave."

The dwarf pulled on his boots, tumbled from the coach, and scurried across the yard toward the inn house.

Alone, Theo tried to set his thoughts in order. He cursed himself for not following Anton and again for not finding him. He put his head in his hands and closed his eyes, only to see the officer's ashen face.

Musket was back. At his heels, a bulky figure was hastily cramming a shirttail into his breeches.

Theo climbed out of the coach. "Dr. Absalom?"

The paunchy man shook his head. He had the plump features of an oversized baby with a ferocious black moustache. "I should say I am at your service, but more likely you shall be at mine. I am Count Las Bombas."

Theo turned to Musket. "I thought you'd gone for Dr. Absalom."

"In the press of circumstances, names are unimportant. They only confuse matters." The count waved a hand, dismissing the question. "My coachman tells me you had some difficulties, and the name 'Absalom' came up, shall we say, in the conversation?"

Theo began his account while Las Bombas nodded encouragement, stopping him occasionally and asking him to repeat certain details.

"The officer, you say, took one of the pages? And kept it?"

Theo nodded. "He called Dr. Absalom a fraud and wanted a closer look at him. After that, when he took out a pistol, I—I think I killed him. I swear it was an accident."

"Heaven help us, then, if you ever do anything on purpose," said Las Bombas. "Now, the two soldiers, did they hear him?"

"They must have. They were standing right there."

"And no doubt will report it to someone, even if their superior is, ah, no longer among us?"

"If they remember," said Theo, "after everything else that happened."

"Inconvenient things are always remembered," said Las Bombas. "We must assume the worst. Wisdom dictates that Dr. Absalom will suddenly be called out of town. As for you, young man, allow me to inquire: What are you going to do to save your neck?"

Theo had been turning over the same question. "I'll have to set things right. I'll go to the police, to the Dorning constabulary."

"The law?" Las Bombas stared at him. "Last place in the world to set things right!"

"What else can I do? My master could be in jail. They had no cause to break into the shop. We did nothing wrong. I meant the officer no harm."

"My dear boy, who's to believe that?"

"It's the truth. They'll have to believe it."

"It is constabulary nature to disbelieve." Count Las Bombas sighed and puffed out his cheeks. "I commend your sense of duty, but have no intention of sharing it. Musket and I shall be leaving directly."

The dwarf, in fact, had been cramming garments into a flexible traveling case. Las Bombas urged him to greater speed, then waved a hand at Theo.

"Farewell. Though I have gravest doubts, I wish a satisfactory resolution to your difficulties."

Leaving the count and his coachman busily packing, Theo made his way across the innyard. He drew the bolt on the gate and slipped out into the street. What had been so clear a choice in the shed now filled him with uneasiness. The count, he feared, might well be right, and a bad affair turn worse. His decision had been the only honorable one. Instead of strengthening him, however, it burdened him. He gritted his teeth and set off for the constabulary.

Before going any distance, he sighted one of the Dorning constables holding a lantern at the end of an alley. Theo called out and went toward him. The constable, after one glimpse, began running in the opposite direction. Having been chased through the streets a good part of the night, the puzzled Theo had to stretch his legs to chase the fleeing officer.

He caught up with him at last. It was Constable Pohn, whom he had known as long as he could remember. Pohn immediately darkened his lantern. Usually good-natured, he rounded angrily on Theo.

"What are you doing here? We've orders to search the town for you."

"Well, you've found me. I was on my way to the station house. Where's Anton? And the officer? Did I—is he alive?"

"He's got a broken head, but he'll mend."

"Thank heaven. What about Anton?"

"There's been a bad piece of business." Pohn took Theo's arm. "Dorning's no place for you."

"I've got to settle things. It was my fault. I don't want Anton blamed."

"He's dead," cried Pohn. "Shot down in the street. They're after you now."

Theo stared, numb. Splinters of ice caught in his throat, choking and tearing him at the same time. Pohn shook him furiously.

"Listen to me! There's an order to arrest you. That was a Royal Inspector you brained. So it's a Crown case, not some local mischief. We can't help you. You can't help Anton.

"You're to be locked up on sight," Pohn hurried on. "But who's to say I saw you? We're going to search the woods west of the river. A wanted criminal—that's where he'd hide, wouldn't he? He'd never take to the open roads. The King's Highway? Last place he'd go. No need wasting our time in that direction. Eh? Eh? Do you understand me?"

Pohn snapped his jaws shut, spun on his heel, and hustled away down the alley, shining his lantern into doorways and corners as if seeking the fugitive in good earnest.

Theo stood bewildered, grasping at fragments of what Pohn had told him. There was no reason, no justice in any of it. With a surge of anger, ignoring the constable's urging, he wanted to stay and face his accuser. Anton had committed no crime, nor had Theo. To leave his only home, his books, his work—yet he knew, with bitterness, it had all suddenly become wreckage.

Painfully, unwilling, he turned and forced his legs to carry him eastward from the town. The sky was lightening. Shreds of mist floated over the market gardens fringing the outskirts of Dorning. A rooster crowed in a farmyard. He pressed on at a faster pace, cutting across newly plowed fields, dimly reckoning he would sooner or later strike the highway.

Only now did the full weight of his grief bear down on him. Along with it was something more, lodged in the back of his mind like a cinder in the eye that could not be wept away.

He could not bring himself to think about it; he could not bring himself to turn away from it. He was unable, finally, to stand it any longer. He admitted what he had hidden from himself and wished to forget.

The frame had not slipped or twisted. It was not an accident. Never in his life had he raised a hand in anger. But in that moment, more than anything else in the world, he had wanted to kill the man.

Until then, he had believed in his own good nature. He pleaded that he was a kindly, honorable human being. But the bloodied face rose up in front of him.

His stomach heaved. He doubled over, retching. He sat on the ground a while, head pressed against his knees. He swore every way he knew: Never again would he do such a deed.

He climbed at last to his feet. The road lay a short distance beyond the field. He set off for it. He did not look back. He did not dare.

∽

4

By midmorning, the sun had burned away the fog from the valley land east of Dorning. Theo calculated he had trudged only a few miles, but he was already weary. He had, thus far, come upon no travelers in either direction, for which he was grateful. Being obliged to give an account of himself was the last thing in the world he wanted. He had already done violence to a man. He did not wish to compound this by doing violence to the truth. He had never told a lie; it occurred to him that sooner or later he would have to lie outrageously. The best he could do was put off the moment as long as possible.

He had begun thinking it might be wiser to stay off the road altogether when he saw a dappled gray mare trotting toward him. Harness leathers trailing, the horse whinnied and tossed her head, but made no objection when he caught the reins and pulled her up. The animal clearly had an owner, but Theo's fatigue outweighed that consideration.

"Hold still, old girl. Whoever you belong to—I'm sorry. I'm a wanted fugitive," he bitterly added. "I might as well be a horse thief, too."

He climbed awkwardly astride. Knowing as much of horsemanship as he did of behaving like a criminal, he nevertheless managed to turn the animal eastward, glad for one piece of good fortune.

His good fortune blistered him before he had ridden a mile. His legs strained. He was footsore where he had no feet. At last, he climbed down and walked. The horse ambled behind him, fondly blowing down the back of his neck, nudging him when his pace slackened.

Before he could decide how to free himself of this animal who was driving him instead of the other way around, he saw, past a bend in the road, a coach pulled onto the grassy shoulder. The doors hung open, some baggage had been spread on the ground, the shafts were empty. On top of the vehicle perched the dwarf, a stubby clay pipe between his teeth. Count Las Bombas, sweating in his shirt-sleeves, sat glumly on a boulder.

Sighting Theo, the dwarf sprang down like an acrobat. "I told you she'd come back one way or another. If you'd let her be, instead of chasing her like an idiot, she wouldn't have run off in the first place."

Las Bombas heaved himself up, nodding at Theo. "I see we have you to thank for finding this ungrateful creature. And so, you changed your mind about reporting yourself to the authorities? Very sensible."

"I would have," Theo began. He faltered, as if saying the words could somehow make it more final than it was. "But—they killed my master."

"I'm sorry, my boy. A hard knock. Where does that leave you?"

"With a warrant out for me. The police as much as ordered me to run away. The Royal Inspector's alive, though."

"And no doubt in better case than we are. Thanks to the roads in your part of the country, a wheel came loose. Then Musket carelessly allowed my steed—Friska! Friska! None of that!"

This was shouted at the horse, nipping at Las Bombas from the rear. The count withdrew to a safe distance while Musket brought the animal to the shafts.

"A civilian beast," the count explained. "Nothing like my charger when I served in the Salamanca Lancers."

Theo had noticed a heap of objects beside the coach and gave a questioning look at what appeared to be a collection of arms and legs.

"Ah, those," said Las Bombas. "Remarkably natural, you must agree. Excellently done." He picked up one of the arms and showed it to Theo. It was hollow, made of painted cloth stretched over a light, flexible wooden frame. "These are often useful in my profession. Sometimes, indeed, essential."

"But your pamphlet said you were a doctor."

"As occasion demands. I have, my boy, spent my life in constant study. Initiate in the Delphic Mysteries, in the Grand Arcana, adviser to His Exalted Serenity, the prince of Trebizonia. I have been instructed by the Great Copta himself in summoning spirits of the dead—with, naturally, a reasonable amount of help from the living."

"You mean," said Theo, "you're no doctor at all."

"Don't take such a narrow view," replied the count. "I assure you, I have lightened more suffering with tubs of magnetized water than most esteemed surgeons have done with lancets and leeches. Those who, for some inscrutable reason, stubbornly refuse to benefit—if I didn't cure them at least I didn't harm them, which cannot be said for a number of your learned bloodletters."

The count reached into his pocket. "It is apparent to me that you suffer from a headache at this very instant. Am I correct?"

Theo's head, in fact, had been throbbing all morning. He admitted this to Las Bombas, who nodded and replied, "I knew it without asking."

He opened his hand, revealing a black pebble the size of an egg. "This, my boy, is worth more than its weight in gold. A priceless fragment from the fabled Mountain of the Moon in Kazanastan. I need only touch it to your brow—thus. Your headache will vanish."

A whistle from Musket interrupted the count. He turned and squinted down the road where the dwarf was pointing. Theo stiffened. A troop of Royal Cavalry was bearing toward them.

"Make a run for it," ordered Las Bombas. "No—that will rouse their suspicions. We'll have to brazen it out."

He rummaged in a pile of clothing and tossed some garments to Theo. "Get behind the coach. Put these on. If there's any question, say you're a Trebizonian."

"I can't speak Trebizonian."

"Neither can they. Very well, you'll be a mute Trebizonian. Get on with it. Not a word out of you. Do as I say."

Theo ducked around the coach and pulled on the costume: a long, striped robe which, by its smell, had not been laundered for years, and a tall, cylindrical headpiece with a tassel.

The troop halted. The captain turned his mount, casting a wary eye on the vehicle. Las Bombas, who had disappeared inside, now climbed out to face the officer. The count was resplendent in a general's gold-braided uniform, its breast glittering with medals.

"What seems to be the difficulty?" blustered the count as the officer sprang down and brought his hand to a rigid salute.

"Beg to report: none, sir." The captain had gone as crimson as the count's uniform. "Forgive me, sir, for disturbing you. My men are going into garrison and I was ordered to keep an eye open along the way. A fugitive from justice, claiming to be a printer's apprentice—"

"What? What?" shouted Las Bombas. "What nonsense are you mumbling? Speak up, sir! Look me in the eye when you address me!"

"A fugitive, sir," blurted the troop captain, "wanted for high crimes."

"Why didn't you say so in the first place?" Las Bombas glared at him. "Well, you don't see anyone like that here, do you? I am General Sambalo, on a special mission from the court."

"Beg to report, sir: I saw an individual near your coach."

"My servant?" The count beckoned to Theo. "This fellow? Trebizonian, as you see. Hardly an apprentice of any sort, eh? Can't speak. Only grunts. I spared his life on my last campaign. He's been devoted to me ever since."

The officer stared at Theo. Las Bombas went on.

"A faithful creature—as far as you can trust any of these savages. Strong as a bull, though you wouldn't think it, looking at him. Poor devil, he's quite mad. Calm and peaceful in the ordinary way of things. What sets him wild is officers with horses. Even I can't control him then."

Taking the count's hint, Theo growled and bared his teeth in what he hoped would pass for a ferocious grimace. Terrified, at the same time he felt himself an utter fool.

"You should have seen what he did to my last aide." Las Bombas gravely shook his head. "Those Trebizonians go straight for the throat, you know."

The troop captain stood at attention, but it was all the man could do to stay there. Las Bombas held the officer with a stern eye, in no hurry to let him escape.

"Have you any money?"

The captain blinked. "Sir?"

"If you do, I suggest giving it to him immediately. It may exercise a calming effect. They understand the offering of money as a gesture of friendship."

The officer pulled out a handful of silver coins and one gold piece from his tunic and flung them at Theo. Las Bombas nodded approval.

"That should hold him. Not long, for such a small amount. Carry on with your duties. I assume the responsibility of watching for the runaway. Dismissed!"

The captain threw a ragged salute, scrambled onto his mount, and plunged back to his men, bawling for them to follow at the gallop.

Las Bombas watched until the troop was well out of sight. He gave Theo a smile of satisfaction. "You made a splendid Trebizonian. For a moment, I thought you were actually going to bite him."

"You got us a gold piece into the bargain," added Musket. "That's pure profit."

"Yes, you pulled it off, my boy," said Las Bombas. "But you had a close call. I confess I sweated a little myself. You might be wise to stay with us for a time. For your own safety. Though it also occurs to me I could use a bright young assistant. The possibilities are unlimited. As to wages, we must leave that question temporarily open."

"No, thank you. It's good of you, but—" Theo hesitated. Until now, he had never imagined himself away from Dorning. The possibility had never existed. With Anton dead and himself homeless, his best course was to stay on the move. The prospect, in fact, excited him, all the more strongly because it was new.

"I doubt if you'll have a better offer," said the count. "Why, you'll launch yourself on an entirely new profession."

The count's profession, Theo knew, was sheer fakery. Las Bombas was a fraud and, worse, proud of it. Nevertheless, against all reason, against all he had read and Anton had taught him, he could not help liking the rogue.

"All right," he said finally. "I'll go with you."

"Excellent!" cried the count. "Pack up and we'll be on our way. Musket will explain your duties."

As soon as the artificial arms and legs and the rest of the baggage had been stowed, Las Bombas rolled himself into the coach. Theo clambered to join Musket on the box. The dwarf clicked his tongue, slapped Friska with the reins, and set off at a speed that took Theo's breath away. With his stubby legs jutting straight in front of him, hat jammed low on his brow and his eyes gleaming, Musket looked every bit a demon coachman. Theo hung on for dear life. The coach swayed and jolted, wind whistled in his ears. What his destination might be, he had no inkling; but they were going there very rapidly. He scarcely noticed his headache had vanished.

5

Cabbarus, chief minister of the realm, bent over his desk scanning a sheaf of documents. Cabbarus had the virtue of diligence with an immense capacity for drudgery, and he had been at his work since dawn. From the day of his elevation from superintendent of the Royal Household, he had shown himself willing and eager to accept duties the other ministers found boring. Cabbarus, as a result, had his fingers in everything from the purchase of lobsters to the signature of death warrants. His eyes were everywhere: eyes the color of slate, unblinking; with a glance that made all on whom it rested feel, in comparison with him, less noble, less high-minded, and that their linen needed changing.

The papers presently under this glance dealt with the latest steps taken against irresponsible pamphleteers and the printers who served them. Cabbarus had not yet received reports from such outlying towns as Belvitsa and Dorning. He expected them shortly. Meantime, he was not displeased.

"The subjects of His Majesty," he was saying, "require the firmest guidance. The people yearn for it, without even realizing what it is they yearn for. These scribblers cause nothing but unrest. Their deaths, beyond question, will serve a higher purpose than their lives: the good of the kingdom. I bear them no personal animosity, but I would fail in my duty if I did otherwise. They will, at least, be spared the needless humiliation of a public trial."

The chief minister's confidential secretary, Councillor Pankratz, made polite growls of approval, no more detailed answer being called for. Pankratz was a head shorter than his master, with enormous calves nearly bursting the stocking of his black court costume. Cabbarus wore no wig to cover the iron gray hair trimmed close to his skull; therefore, his secretary dared not wear one. The courtiers had nicknamed Pankratz The Minister's Mastiff. Among themselves, they joked that while Cabbarus was preaching at his listeners, Pankratz was biting their legs.

Time had come for the morning audience with King Augustine. Cabbarus ordered his mastiff to pack the documents in a red leather box. With Pankratz trotting two paces behind, Cabbarus left his quarters and made his way across the courtyard to the newer wings of the palace. These splendid areas had been raised by the king's grandfather, the second Augustine, now called The Great.

The original Juliana Palace had been an ancient fortress of thick stone walls, narrow passages, dungeons, and torture chambers. Instead of tearing down the historic structure, Augustine the Great built around and added to it. In one of the watchtowers he installed the famous Juliana Bells. Their peal set the mood of the city, as if they were the voice of Marianstat itself. Augustine IV had commanded them to remain forever silent, in perpetual mourning for the late Princess Augusta. The child had loved them. The king found them too-painful reminders of his daughter. He preferred muteness to memory.

Most of the Old Juliana had been given over to storage and the offices of lower functionaries. Cabbarus had lived and worked there during his superintendency. As chief minister, he was entitled to sumptuous chambers in the New Juliana. He declined them. He kept his same quarters, setting an example of frugality and modesty; righteousness being always more believable when combined with dreariness.

Since Augustine no longer received ministers in the audience chamber, Cabbarus went directly to the king's apartments. Taking the red box from his secretary, he allowed himself to be ushered in. Pankratz stationed himself outside the door, keeping a dog's eye on the attendants in the hall.

The apartments were airless and stifling hot. Draperies blinded the casements. Spring had come early and warm, but logs blazed in the fireplace. Cabbarus set down his box on a side table and approached the king. Augustine, in a dressing gown, sat in a high-backed chair close to the fire. He barely acknowledged the presence of his chief minister.

"I trust Your Majesty slept well," said Cabbarus, knowing the king seldom slept more than an hour at a time.

Augustine turned a feverish eye on his chief minister. The king was not a tall man; since his loss, he had shrunk still further into himself: emptied, filled only with inner shadows. He had never ceased to blame himself for being too doting a father. Had he been less indulgent, the tragedy would not have happened. Because it was too late to take a stronger hand with his daughter, he had chosen Cabbarus to take a stronger hand with his people. Since then, Augustine had only one concern.

"Have you still found none with the true gift?" asked the king. "Those who can summon the spirits of the dead?"

Cabbarus stifled a sigh. He had hoped that Augustine, for once, would not bring up the matter. "Your Majesty has always been disappointed."

"I charge you to find one who will not disappoint me. I will speak with my daughter. Let her spirit come to me, even from her unknown grave."

"Sire, your duty is toward the living." Cabbarus did not intend pursuing this old and tiresome subject. He did not even intend discussing the contents of the box. The topic he resolved to raise this morning, as it had grown in his mind, filled him with a pleasure he would have judged indecent had it not been directed toward the good of the kingdom.

Augustine had given him the opening he sought, and he hurried on before he lost the monarch's attention. "Indeed, Sire, kings have a duty even beyond the tomb. We are all, at the end, dust and ashes. Your Majesty, alas, bears the added burden of determining his successor."

"There is no successor."

"Precisely my point, Majesty. Queen Caroline, as a royal widow, may rule in your stead. This merely delays the question without resolving it. Your Majesty must have an heir to carry on his sacred trust."

Augustine frowned. "It is no longer possible."

"Permit me to say, Majesty: on the contrary. It is both possible and urgent. The law permits you to adopt one. It requires only your decree, confirmed by the assent of Queen Caroline."

"Are you saying, Chief Minister, that the Queen and I should adopt a daughter?"

"Not a daughter," Cabbarus replied, "joyful as that might be. Not a daughter, Majesty, a son. A son who dreams, who hopes, who will strive to approach the wisdom, strength, and vision of his glorious, though adoptive, forebears. A son who will honor Your Majesty now and in the years to come—"

"Speak of this another time," said Augustine. "I am weary. There is, moreover, none I would consider."

"None?" cried Cabbarus, dropping to his knees. "Majesty, let me reveal to you the respect, the affection, the love that has grown daily within my heart, the dream of that glorious day when I may call you Father!"

It took the king a moment to understand his chief minister's proposal. He staggered to his feet. "You? In the place of my dead child?"

The king struggled to disengage himself from the embrace of his chief minister. Cabbarus, in turn, did all he could to cling to the legs of his prospective parent. Augustine's face went gray. He stretched out his hands, groping vaguely, and toppled to the floor.

In despair, not at the king's possibly fatal collapse but its untimeliness, Cabbarus seized the monarch's wrist. The pulse beat faintly. Cabbarus climbed to his feet, flung open the door, and shouted for help. He returned to the prostrate Augustine and stood wringing his hands.

Queen Caroline was there in moments. Hardly glancing at Cabbarus, she knelt beside her husband and loosened his gown and shirt. The queen still wore mourning, as she had done for six years past. While the king's grief had weakened him, her grief had only strengthened her. Despite her anxiety, her features were sternly controlled. When Cabbarus tried to speak, she cut him off with a gesture and followed the attendants who bore Augustine to a couch.

"Madam," protested Cabbarus, "we had scarcely begun our audience. His Majesty appeared in better case than when I left him yesterday."

"His Majesty," replied the queen, "is in even better case when you are absent."

The court physician had now entered and was ordering the attendants, including Pankratz, to take themselves off. Dr. Torrens was still in his shirtsleeves. His face, broad and blunt, was softened by a mane of silver hair, unpowdered, caught at the back by a common cotton ribbon.

"Madam, I must ask you to withdraw," said Torrens, adding to Cabbarus, "and you, too."

Cabbarus glowered at the court physician. The queen went to the antechamber and sank down on a chair. Cabbarus reluctantly followed. Since the queen did not give him leave to sit, he took up a station in the middle of the room, his head bowed, hands clasped before him. Thus the queen and the chief minister shared close quarters and chilly silence until Torrens reappeared.

"The king is sleeping now, a blessing in itself," he said to the queen. Dr. Torrens finished rolling down his sleeves, then addressed Cabbarus. "He has had a severe shock. You were with him, Chief Minister. I think you shall have to answer for it."

"I would not call it shock," said Cabbarus, looking past Torrens to the queen. "Rather say, Madam, an excess of joy. His Majesty was discussing the happy prospect of adopting a son and heir. His fondest wish, his royal choice devolved upon—" Cabbarus sighed and spread his hands. "Myself. Public duty and personal devotion led me to accept this highest honor. For the king, the joyous excitement of that moment—"

"How dare you!" cried the queen. "How dare you speak of yourself as adoptive heir? Such a question is raised privately, between the king and me. The queen's consent is required first and foremost, as you well know. That consent, I assure you, will never be given. I desire Dr. Torrens, here and now, to witness my refusal."

"Privately or publicly, Madam, the question must be raised," answered Cabbarus. "The king is desperately ill."

"Yes," put in Torrens, "but I can also tell you the king has no illness. Not in the physical sense. His body is wasted and weakened. This might be set right, as I have tried to do; and would have done, except for the meddling of idiots like you, who set my regimens aside. The king's body may answer to common-sense treatment, to food, sleep, and fresh air. His gravest illness lies in his spirit."

"You are saying the king is mad!" exclaimed Cabbarus. "This is high treason. You are more than incompetent, you are a traitor!"

"Neither one nor the other," Torrens answered. "The king is not mad. He is sick with grief, frozen in self-blame. No, I am not a traitor. I am a man who speaks his mind and faces facts." He turned to the queen. "Do not lose hope. His Majesty may, in time, recover. Meanwhile, I urge you, allow him to make no decisions he may come to regret, and certainly not the adoption of—"

"You go too far!" Cabbarus burst out. "Your trade is physic, not affairs of state. The king must and will follow the guidance of his ministers."

"Forgive me," said Torrens. "I called you an idiot. I spoke hastily. You are not. Had I given it more thought, I would have called you a scoundrel." He bowed to the queen. "Your servant, Madam."

Dr. Torrens turned on his heel and strode from the chamber. Queen Caroline hurried after him. Cabbarus, about to follow and give Torrens a withering reply, thought better of it and remained there, silent.

The chief minister enjoyed a gift for sniffing out possibilities without immediately understanding them.

As before, when he had trusted this instinct, nothing could have been foreseen. He had risen, nevertheless, to chief minister. When the proper moment came, there would be many in the Royal Council to favor him as adoptive heir. As for Torrens, he would be dealt with. A plan was already shaping in his mind. It always pleased the chief minister how clear-sighted he could be in clouded circumstances.

6

The Demon Coachman brought them to Kessel: hungry, late, and sopping wet. The morning repairs had not outlasted the day, the wheel threatened to come off again at any moment, and a spring rainstorm had begun pelting down. Taking the risk of sending coach and passengers into a ditch, Musket pressed ahead, hunched on the box, whistling through his teeth, grinning like an undersized fiend in an oversized hat.

Kessel offered a large inn. Because of the storm, however, it looked as if every traveler had broken his journey there. The common room stank of wet clothing and bad cooking. Las Bombas, Musket and Theo following, elbowed his way to the chimney corner and called loudly for the host. The count, in the privacy of the coach, had changed from his uniform into garments of black set off by white wristbands.

"The chambers of Mynheer Bloomsa and servants," declared Las Bombas when the landlord finally appeared. "You have my message reserving them."

The landlord, taken aback by the sight of the Demon Coachman and a dripping Trebizonian, protested that no such message had come. In any case, his house was full. Theo, having digested his surprise at the count's new role, expected Las Bombas to make a show of indignation.

The count merely sighed. "That's the public post for you. It is not your fault. I required a suite of your finest apartments, but I shall have to seek accommodation elsewhere."

Instead of doing so, Las Bombas stood casting an eye over the travelers. When Theo urged him to leave before it would be too late to find another inn, Las Bombas shrugged him off.

"Patience, my boy. I'm looking for pigeons. You might oblige me by handing over that gold piece, temporarily."

Theo gave him the captain's coin, which Las Bombas quickly pocketed. His attention meanwhile had settled on a table occupied by a plump little man in a fur-trimmed cloak. The count made his way toward him. Passing the table, he contrived to pull out his handkerchief so that the gold piece dropped to the floor. Las Bombas kept on as if he had not noticed.

"Good sir, your money!" the man called after him, picking up the coin.

The count turned back and allowed the traveler to press it into his hand. "You need not have troubled yourself, sir. It is of no account. I thank you, nevertheless."

"Permit me"—the traveler popped his watery, pink-rimmed eyes at the count—"permit me to remark: I would hardly call gold of no account. My name is Skeit, alderman and corn merchant, and I assure you, sir, in my occupation I know the value of money."

"I, too," replied Las Bombas, with an appraising glance at the quality of the alderman's garb and the weight of the gold chain he wore as ornament. "To me, its value is precisely nothing."

"My good Mynheer!" cried the alderman. "Bloomsa, was that the name I overheard? You amaze me!"

"No doubt I do." The count beamed. "Money, my dear sir, is only metal and, like any other substance, subject to the same natural laws of transmutation and transmogrification. I am a man of science, not finance." He lowered his voice and drew closer to Skeit. "My experiments have brought me the means of creating as much gold and silver as I please. Therefore, whatever value they may have for others, for me they have none."

"But—but this is marvelous! My journey has been most profitable, but nothing compared with meeting a personage of your accomplishment. Wait until my good wife hears of this when I'm home!"

"Since you have troubled yourself on my behalf," said Las Bombas, "allow me to offer you supper before I leave. I must find some lodging still available at this dismal time of night."

"Indeed, not!" returned Skeit. "I shall be the one to offer you supper. Look no further, I insist you share my own quarters."

"If it pleases you," said Las Bombas. "My servants can take their food in the stables, while they attend to my horse and coach."

The count, during this, was gesturing urgently behind his back. Musket pulled Theo out of the common room and hustled him to the stable.

"What was that all about?" asked Theo, as the dwarf tossed him some rags and a brush to wipe down Friska. "He's up to some trickery. The man doesn't have an honorable bone in his body."

A powerful kick sent Theo into a pile of straw: not from Friska, but from the dwarf, who stood, hands on hips, glowering at him.

"Mind your tongue," said Musket, "next time you have anything to say about the count."

"It's true, isn't it?" cried Theo.

"What if it is? I'll hear nothing against the man who bought me. That's right," Musket went on. "How much he paid, or if he swindled them out of the price, I don't know or care. I was half your age. In Napolita. He bought me from the beggar factory."

"From the—what?"

"Beggar factory," the dwarf said cheerfully. "No, you wouldn't have heard of that in your little hole-and-corner. But you've never wondered why there's so many beggars? Oh, there's no shortage of first-rate paupers, lame, halt, and blind. But half your noseless, or legless, or hunchbacked—they've been custom-tailored for the trade. Youngsters bought or stolen, then broken past mending, sliced up, squeezed into jars to make them grow crooked. Sold off to a master who pockets whatever charity's thrown to them."

"That's horrible. It can't be true."

"Can't be," said Musket. "But is. I was lucky. I was born like this, no adjustments required. If it hadn't been the count who bought me, no telling where I'd be. Rascal he is, but he's a good-natured one. Take your nobles who flog their servants, gouge their tenants, or the judges who send some wretch to be hanged—they're honest as the day is long. Any scoundrel can be honest."

"But all the rest of it," said Theo. "The Salamanca Lancers! Great Copta! Trebizonia—I wonder if he even knows where it is. Why does he put out such nonsense?"

"No business of mine," said Musket. "For all I know, he can't stomach the world as he finds it. Can you?"

Theo did not answer. He turned back to rubbing down Friska. He had been more comfortable when he had been able to judge Las Bombas a complete rogue.

The potboy brought them supper. Since it was too

late to rouse a blacksmith, Musket and Theo set about repairing the wheel themselves. The dwarf, this time, swore his work would last. Soon after they finished, the count hurried into the stable.

"Master Skeit's on his way home," said Las Bombas, smiling like a cream-sodden cat. "But he'll be back, looking for us. We'd best be off." He triumphantly held up a knotted handkerchief that chinked as he shook it.

"I have performed an experiment in elementary alchemy. My coins, I assured our good alderman, had a remarkable quality. They could multiply any others they touched, as easily as a hen hatching eggs. He had only to wrap his money up with mine and let it brood overnight. By morning, he'd have treble his fortune.

"He was overjoyed. We set the packet on the mantel in his chamber and went to bed. It couldn't have turned out better. He woke up, restless; he wanted to get home with his fortune. I warned him not to undo the handkerchief till dawn, or the experiment would fail. But he won't wait; he's too greedy. When he sees what he has, he'll turn back on the instant.

"What I forgot to tell him was while he was snoring away, I tied up another kerchief with nothing but pebbles in it, and changed it for the one on the mantel."

"You robbed him!" cried Theo. "You might as well have held a pistol to his head."

"Nonsense," replied Las Bombas. "I don't carry a pistol. My dear boy, until I can set Dr. Absalom to work again, this money's the only thing to put food in our mouths."

Chuckling, Las Bombas unknotted the handkerchief. Then he choked and stared. His face went mottled. There was only a handful of leaden disks.

"Slugs!" roared Las Bombas. "He switched the packets! But—I had my eye on the real one every second. I never left his side, only when he was fast asleep and I went out to the yard for pebbles. I wasn't gone a minute—That wretch! He was shamming! Robber! How dare he pass himself off as an alderman!"

The count ran to the stable door and shook his fist into the night. "Villain! Little sneak!"

He turned back to Theo. "Ah, my poor lad, there's a lesson for you. Never trust a stranger. What a world, with so many thieves abroad in it."

PART TWO
The Oracle Priestess

&

❧

7

Las Bombas, as Theo began to learn, could not stay long in low spirits. By the time Musket had Friska between the shafts and the coach ready to roll, the count's storm of indignation had passed, and he was eager to set off.

"Our fortune has been frayed," he told Theo, "but we shall mend it thread by thread."

The Demon Coachman, chewing on his pipestem, let Friska make her own pace, ambling eastward. Toward afternoon, they came in sight of a town, which the count identified as Born. He ordered Musket to halt in a vacant lot on the outskirts.

"There's a good supply of ditch water," said Las Bombas, surveying the weed-choked field. "Plenty for Dr. Absalom's Elixir. As a further attraction, I think we shall do The Goblin in the Bottle."

"No you don't," put in Musket. "No more of that."

"The effect is marvelous," the count said to Theo. "A glass bottle with a head inside that answers every question about the future. Musket sits under a table with a hole in it, the bottle has a false bottom—"

"Yes, and last time some wiseacre corked me up. I could have smothered. No more, that's flat." Musket snapped his jaws shut and folded his arms.

Las Bombas shrugged and went on. "In any case, we'll have The Unfortunate Child of Nature. It goes with Dr. Absalom's Elixir. You," he added to Theo, "will be an untamed savage from the wilds of High Brazil—whooping, leaping about, whatever occurs to you. One drink of elixir—you needn't swallow it—and you're calm and happy as a lark. You made a splendid Trebizonian. The Unfortunate Child of Nature is the same, except for the blue and yellow stripes."

"I can't paint my clothes," replied Theo. "They're all I have."

"Not your clothes, yourself. As for clothes, you'll need very few."

Las Bombas produced a dented bugle from the chest at the back of the coach and sent Musket with it into Born to announce their presence. He set out some paintpots and instructed Theo, who had reluctantly stripped to his undergarments, in the art of becoming the Unfortunate Child of Nature. While Theo daubed himself, Las Bombas filled a number of glass phials at the ditch, adding powdered herbs from his own supply. For his costume, he donned a shabby robe, a wig, and pair of spectacles. Finally, he attached four rods to the corners of a box lid and on this makeshift table put a life-sized wooden head.

"A phrenological head," explained the count. "It shows the location of humors, dispositions, and temperaments. My patients, for some reason, find it reassuring."

Musket had come back, blaring his bugle, trailed by a straggle of idlers and street urchins. Las Bombas began to proclaim the virtues of Dr. Absalom's Elixir, and Theo to offer his best version of a High Brazilian war dance. Neither got far in these occupations.

"Welcome, fellow blockheads," declared the phrenological head.

Las Bombas choked in midsentence. Theo's war
whoop died on his lips. The voice had come from the
wooden head.

"Come on, don't be shy," it continued. "Have a taste
of that mess. Look what it did for me. I rubbed some
on my hair. Now I save a fortune in barbering."

The onlookers burst into laughter, taking these remarks as part of the show.

"I'll thank you not to interrupt," said the count,
hastily collecting his wits and trying to behave as if he
had expected this to happen. "Please hold your
tongue, sir. Or madam. Whichever you are."

The phrenological head answered with a loud, wet,
and rasping noise, adding, "At your age, can't you tell
the difference?"

The impudence of the head and the discomfort of
Las Bombas sent the crowd into new gales of laughter. Some of the onlookers began tossing coins onto
the table. This encouraged the head to inquire if there
were moths in the count's wig, to comment on the size
of his paunch, and the uselessness of his lazy assis-
tants. The audience guffawed, more coins sailed
through the air. When it was clear that the onlookers
had emptied their pockets, the phrenological head announced it had nothing more to say. Las Bombas had
sold not one bottle of elixir, but the profits were as
great as if he had fobbed off his entire stock.

Once the audience had drifted away, the count
seized the phrenological head, turned it upside down,
shook it, and rapped it with his knuckles.

"Speak up! What's the trick?"

Meantime, one of the urchins crept from under the
coach and stood watching them. It took Theo a moment to realize this collection of skin and bones was a
girl. She wore a pair of ragged breeches tied with a

rope about her bony hips, and a dirty shirt with more
holes than cloth. She was drab as a street sparrow,
with a beaky nose in a narrow face. Her eyes were
blue, but pale as if the color had been starved out of
them.

Theo had never seen such a pitiful waif. The count,
however, was less deeply touched.

"Off with you," Las Bombas ordered. "We are conducting a scientific investigation."

"Give her something. You can see she's hungry."
Without waiting for the count's approval, Theo picked
a coin from the table. The waif snatched it and held
out a filthy palm.

"Let's have my share. You wouldn't have peddled a
drop of that muck without me, not to that crowd."

"What are you saying?" demanded the count. "That
you did all the nonsense?"

"Cough it up," declared the phrenological head.
"Pay out fair and square or I'll never speak another
word."

Las Bombas gaped. "Do that again."

"You heard me the first time."

The voice came from inside the coach. Startled,
Theo turned to look. Las Bombas had not taken his
eyes from the girl's lips. He studied her closely with
genuine admiration.

"In all my travels, I've only met three people better
at that trick. Who taught you?"

"Nobody. I learned it myself, when I was in the
Queen's Home for Repentant Girls. The charity mistress wouldn't let us talk to each other. So I used to
send her into fits. She never knew who to blame. She
must have been glad when I escaped."

"And you've been living on your own, in the
streets?" put in Theo, dismayed.

"Hanno was my friend for a while. He was a burglar—the best. He said I could be as good as he was.

He was teaching me the trade," the girl added proudly. "Then he got hanged."

The dwarf had finished collecting the stray coins. The girl looked him up and down. "Hallo there, Thumbling. Give us a pull on your pipe."

The dwarf grinned and handed it over. She squatted down, stretched out her legs and, to Theo's further distress, puffed away happily. The urchin luxuriously scratched her washboard of ribs through the holes in her shirt.

"Now," she said, "where's the rest of my money?"

Las Bombas did not answer immediately. His eyes seemed fixed on some distant vision. He smiled with a look of pure greed and innocent joy.

"My dear lady," he said at last, "whatever your name is—"

"Mickle is what they call me."

"Mickle, then. I take it you have no permanent attachments. I urge you to join me and my colleagues. The possibilities are vast. The sums could be enormous."

"Sums?" said Mickle. "Does that mean money?"

"All you could desire. Eventually, that is."

"Done!" cried Mickle, spitting in her palm and seizing the count's hand. Theo could not keep silent.

"Wait a minute," he said to Las Bombas. "You can't just pick her up like a stray cat. She ought to be someplace where she can be looked after properly. It's not fair to the girl—"

"He was talking to me, not you," broke in Mickle. "You stay out of it with your 'It's not fair to the girl, she ought to be looked after properly.'"

The girl had spoken these last words in Theo's own voice. Though lighter in tone, the accents were identical. Theo did not find it flattering.

Las Bombas clapped his hands. "Marvelous! Still another gift! We'll find good use for it."

Theo said no more, knowing it would be labor lost. He was, moreover, unwilling to open his mouth and have his words tossed back into it. He smarted at the girl's mimicry. He went to the ditch and set about washing off the paint.

When Theo returned, Las Bombas announced they would travel no further that day. Musket hurried into Born to buy provisions. Mickle flung herself on the food, gobbled it as if it could be snatched away at any moment, wiped her hands on her breeches, and contentedly sucked her teeth. At nightfall, Las Bombas opened one of the coach seats, turning it into a cot, and bedded down on it. Musket curled up on the box while Theo stretched out under the coach. Mickle sprawled on the turf beside Friska.

The moon was still high when Theo woke to a thin, trembling sound, like a small animal in pain. He listened a moment. It came from the direction of Friska and the girl. He crawled out and walked cautiously toward them. The mare switched her tail and snuffled gently. Mickle lay on her side, one arm beneath her head, the other outflung. She was motionless, but sobbing as if her heart would break.

Alarmed, Theo knelt. "What's the matter?"

The girl did not answer. Tears flooded her cheeks. He waited silently a while, then went back to the coach. The girl had never stirred. Through all her weeping, she had been fast asleep.

8

By the time Theo opened his eyes, Las Bombas was already up and stirring, dressed in an embroidered caftan and red fez.

"There you are, awake at last," said the count while Theo climbed stiffly to his feet. "Great plans are in store. We'll talk them over at breakfast. I'll pack away Dr. Absalom's Elixir. I suggest you go and rouse our young lady. She'll be in your charge. Your first responsibility, on the earliest occasion, will be to make certain she takes a bath. She's a natural genius, but she smells like a fox."

Mickle still sprawled on the turf. Twice during the night, Theo had gone anxiously to her side. Except for that one strange spell of weeping, she had slept peacefully as she slept now, a half-smile on her wan face. Reluctant to wake her, for some moments he looked down at the girl, feeling like an eavesdropper on a secret part of her life. At last, he took her by the shoulders and gently shook her.

"Come along. It's morning."

"Go away," mumbled the girl. "I get up at noon."

Theo continued urging, but what finally brought Mickle to her feet was the aroma of eggs which Musket was frying in a saucepan. While she attacked her breakfast, the count polished the lens of a lantern, then set it down beside several large round looking glasses.

"The tools to fame and fortune," said the count. "Oh, we'll do The Phrenological Head, I have some further thoughts on that. But what I have in mind is far more spectacular: The Undine. That's a mermaid, my dear, half human, half fish. A fabulous creature of the sea, charming, alluring. Picture it. A dimly lit chamber—we'll use the lantern for that. The Undine seeming to float in midair—I've worked out a clever arrangement of those mirrors. The beautiful sea-child speaks. She knows all. She reveals the mysteries of the future. At a good fee, of course. For a costume, she only needs a fishtail. Any seamstress can stitch it up."

The count beamed. "There's my plan. Simple, elegant, and cheap. What do you say to that?"

Mickle shrugged. "It's easier than housebreaking."

"If you ask me," said Theo, "I think it's nonsense."

"My dear boy!" Las Bombas gave him a wounded glance. "How can you say—"

"Look at her," Theo went on. "Who'll pay to see a scrawny little street bird decked out as a mermaid?" This was his honest, but less than complete, opinion. For some reason, the idea of Mickle being gawked at gave him a peculiar twinge.

Las Bombas drew himself up in injured pride. "No doubt you have a better suggestion."

"Yes, well—in fact, I do," Theo declared. Having made this claim, he wondered how to justify it. He paused, hastily seeking an idea, then went on. "Didn't you tell me something about summoning spirits?"

"They proved reluctant," the count admitted. "In other words, I couldn't pull it off."

"Now you can. Put those arms and legs together with the phrenological head. Dress the girl in a black robe and hood, at a table with one candle in front of her. The spirit appears out of thin air—Musket and I can pull it up and down on strings—and seems to talk. You know she's good at that."

The count said nothing for a long moment. His face shone, his moustache quivered, and he whispered in a voice filled with awe. "The Oracle Priestess. I can see her now. Marvelous!"

"We have paints and brushes," added Theo. "I can make a signboard announcing it."

Las Bombas turned a smile of admiration on Theo. "My boy, I'm proud of you. You have the mind of a first-rate mountebank."

The count, on the spot, produced a square of pasteboard from his store of oddments and ordered Theo to begin work immediately.

Collecting his drawing materials, Theo sat on the ground a little distance away and began to sketch the letters, sorry Anton had ever taught him the skill. He had only intended to keep Las Bombas from making a spectacle of the girl; instead, he had put the count onto a scheme equally disreputable. The count's compliment had unsettled him further. He wondered if indeed he had the heart of a mountebank. He already knew he could have been a murderer.

Mickle had been circling him, venturing closer until she was able to peer over his shoulder. "What's it say there?"

Having put himself into his predicament entirely by his own efforts, Theo was out of sorts with everyone else, especially the girl. "It's plain enough, isn't it?"

Mickle shook her head. "I don't know letters."

"You can't write?" Theo put down his brush. "You can't even read?"

"I wanted to. Nobody would teach me. Hanno said it was a waste of time for a burglar. In the home, they mostly gave us repentance and oatmeal. So I never learned."

"Didn't your parents teach you?"

"They couldn't."

"Couldn't read or write, either?"

"I don't know. They were dead. I don't even remember them. I used to live with my grandfather until he died, too. Now I'll never learn."

"Yes, you will." Theo forgot he was supposed to be vexed. "It's easy. I can show you, for a start. Right now. Do you want to?"

Mickle nodded. Theo put aside the poster and picked up a sheet of paper. Mickle crouched beside him, eyes wide.

"We'll begin with block letters." Theo plied his brush. "Look here. This is the first: A."

"I've heard of that. So that's what it looks like?"

"Remember now: A stands for *apple*."

"What?" cried Mickle. "I know apples. That isn't one."

"It's only for the sound," said Theo. "All right. Make it A for—for *arrowhead*."

"That's better. Yes, I can see that."

"Then comes B. It's a *boat*, with wind in the sails. Now, for C—"

"How long do they go on?" protested Mickle. "Just tell me the best ones."

"You'll have to know them all, twenty-six of them."

The girl whistled. "That many? I don't have to use them all at once, do I?"

"Of course not. But when you go to write a word, you have to do it letter by letter."

"That's a slow business. I know something faster." Mickle made small, quick gestures with her fingers.

"That's how my grandfather and I used to talk. He was deaf and dumb, you see. I worked it out better after I ran off. When they caught me and put me in the home, I showed the other girls how to do it. The charity mistress didn't know we were talking. She thought we were only fidgeting. Then, with Hanno, we made up all kinds of signals. Just lifting your knuckle—like this—it meant 'Look out, someone's coming.' In the burglar trade, it helps if you can talk without making noise."

"Will you teach me?"

"Why? Are you going in for burgling?"

"I like to learn things, that's all. Come on, I'll make a bargain with you. Teach me your language and I'll teach you numbers as well as letters."

"All right," said Mickle. "But no skimping. Show me all twenty-six. And all the numbers, too."

The paint had begun to cake. Promising to go on with the lesson as soon as he finished, Theo turned back to his work. Mickle stayed beside him, watching closely.

After a time, he turned to her and asked quietly, "Are you all right now?"

The girl frowned. "What do you mean?"

"You were crying last night."

"Was not! I never cried in all my life. Not when my granddad died, not when the mistress strapped me, not even when Hanno—"

"I heard you," said Theo. "I saw you. You must have been having a bad dream."

The girl drew back and jumped to her feet. She did not answer, only darted to the coach. Theo called after her. She paid no attention. Las Bombas was urging him to finish quickly so they could be on their way. Theo's hand trembled and he blotted a letter.

9

Cabbarus was happy. Going about his duties, he paced the corridors of the Juliana with his head bowed, the corners of his mouth turned down. Following His Majesty's collapse, the chief minister had suffered some uneasy moments. If the prospect of Cabbarus for a son had been enough to bring on a seizure, Augustine, recuperating, might have dismissed him outright. On the contrary, the king needed him more than ever, and refused to see any other councillor. And so Cabbarus was happy. As a principle, he tried only to show feelings admirably grave. Pankratz alone understood that his master's morose frown and air of aggressive gloom indicated that Cabbarus was in the best of spirits.

The desired state of affairs had come about very simply. Dr. Torrens had refused to bleed the king, to purge him, blister him with poultices, or dose him with potions. To the dismay of the chief minister, Augustine regained some of his health.

As Torrens admitted, it was health only of the body. The king spent his new energy pursuing his old obses-

sion. Cabbarus had no intention of turning him from
it. Instead of warning him against disappointment,
Cabbarus provided Augustine with still more occultists and spiritualists, each with a different method of
summoning the departed. They shared one thing in
common: failure. Each disappointment took its toll of
Augustine's health, undoing the best efforts of the
court physician.

Dr. Torrens was furious. He entreated the king to
give up a ruinous, futile quest. Cabbarus, naturally,
sided with the king. By serving his monarch's desires,
which was no less than his sacred duty, Cabbarus set
His Majesty and the court physician at loggerheads: a
situation that grew more bitter each day.

The storm broke sooner than Cabbarus hoped. It
followed an audience granted to the latest necroman-
cer, a hairless little man in tinted spectacles: a fraud
who actually believed in his nonexistent gift and was
sincerely dismayed when he could raise no spirits at
all. He left the king on the brink of new collapse.

Dr. Torrens had word of it within the hour. He
burst into the royal apartments unsummoned, unannounced. The king, pale and shaking, slumped in his
chair. Cabbarus sprang to defend the patient against
his doctor.

"You have no business here," declared Cabbarus,
holding off the angry Torrens. "His Majesty is suffering."

Torrens addressed himself bluntly to Augustine.
"Sire, I have warned you against the consequences of
dealing with these charlatans. As your physician, I
insist—"

"You shall insist upon nothing," broke in Cabbarus.
"The tender emotions of a bereaved father, indeed of
a royal father, do not fall within your competence."

"Grief is not only the privilege of kings," said Torrens, disregarding the chief minister. "We all have a right to it. But enough is enough. Your Majesty has made progress. I will not see my work destroyed by quackery."

"If your work can be destroyed so easily," said Cabbarus, "then your methods, Doctor, are ineffective to begin with. His Majesty has been disappointed, for one simple reason. The inducements have not been sufficient to attract those of highest ability. We have agreed—is that not correct, Your Highness?—to offer a more substantial sum. The individual who enables His Majesty to communicate with the late princess will receive the highest reward."

"Call it bait," replied Torrens. "Every knave in the kingdom will try for it. The greater the sum, the greater the knave. As you, Chief Minister, appreciate better than anyone. Sire, have you agreed to this?"

King Augustine's lips moved, but the words were too faint to be heard.

"His Majesty says he fully agrees," declared Cabbarus. "He desires to speak with you no further."

Dr. Torrens was not famous in the Juliana for sparing anyone the rough side of his tongue, but he said with unusual gentleness, "Majesty, none of us knows what lies beyond the tomb. I can only tell you this: Death is not unfamiliar to me. I have seen more of it than I wish. Disease, accident—the forms are different, the end is the same. What befalls us afterward is a mystery. Death is a fact. Forgive me, Sire, if I wound you, but the princess is dead. Unless you accept that simple fact, you will be prey to every false hope."

Augustine's face twisted in anguish. "No! She will return!"

"Majesty, I must forbid any further exertion in these useless—"

"You will forbid nothing!" cried Cabbarus. "Do you dare stand between a father and his daughter?"

"Yes!" flung back Torrens. "Yes! By heaven, Cabbarus, I shall do all in my power to end this folly."

"Your Highness, do you hear the fellow?" Cabbarus recoiled in shock and indignation. "The truth at last! He admits it. He works against you. A loyal subject would seek only to reunite you and the princess, however briefly. What, then, are we to think of one who desires the opposite?"

Cabbarus stretched out an accusing finger at the court physician. "You have gone too far. You are dismissed from His Majesty's service. Banished from the kingdom. Return at your peril, under pain of death. Be grateful your punishment is so light."

"These are your words, not the king's. You have done your best to make a puppet of him, and have done all too well." The court physician was a vigorous man with the arms and shoulders of a peasant. He pushed Cabbarus aside and dropped to one knee before Augustine.

"I beg you, Sire, listen to me. You risk your life and sanity for no purpose. This villain puts words in your mouth. Speak for yourself."

Augustine's lips trembled, but the words were clear. "We banish you. Set foot again in our kingdom and your life is forfeit. Such is our Royal Will."

Torrens drew back as if the king had struck him.

Cabbarus folded his arms. "I would say, Dr. Torrens, you have been answered."

There was, as the chief minister had long observed, a noose to fit every neck. The court physician had found his with very little guidance. It had been easier than Cabbarus expected.

In his apartments, Dr. Torrens finished packing a few surgical instruments and personal belongings he would carry with him. He turned at the sound of his door opening. It was Queen Caroline.

If the court physician was surprised to see her in his quarters, he was more concerned to see her so distraught. It was not the queen's custom to give way to visible emotion, but all her will could not keep her hands from trembling. Dr. Torrens bowed and gave a wry smile of apology for the disordered chamber.

"As you gather, Madam, I have been obliged to deal with the inconveniences of a hasty departure. The chief minister has already prepared a warrant for my execution. He has the satisfaction of seeing me exiled. I prefer not to give him the pleasure of seeing me hanged."

"I feared you had left the palace," Queen Caroline said. "This is despicable. Even a common criminal is granted more time to set his affairs in order."

Torrens laughed. "To Cabbarus I am a most uncommon criminal. I spoke the truth to His Majesty. In any case, I would not have gone without taking leave of you and explaining my side of it. Cabbarus will no doubt spread his own version."

"He has done so, and of course I did not believe it. I went immediately to the king. He refused to see me. I was unable to help you. Thus His Majesty loses his strongest friend."

"Not altogether."

"How not? Most of the ministers do as Cabbarus orders, the rest hold their tongues. When you go, the king's one strength goes with you. Cabbarus has played his hand cleverly."

"A scoundrel is no more clever than an honest man; he only works harder at it. He has not won all the stakes."

The queen gave him a questioning look.

Dr. Torrens went on. "My baggage will soon be taken to the port. I have ordered inquiries made of vessels ready to sail; the more remote their destination, the better."

"Must you go so far? There are closer kingdoms where you would be safe."

"I spoke of my baggage, not myself. I do not intend leaving Westmark. I shall try to send you word as often as I can. It may not always be possible. If you hear nothing from me, assume the best. Or the worst. In either case, do not lose heart. You and His Majesty have yet another strength. I will seek it out and do all I can to nourish it. In time, it may prove the strongest. I speak, Madam, of the people of Westmark."

"Our subjects? But how, then—"

"I said 'people,' Madam. They are your subjects through affection and loyalty. They are people in their own right. I believe most understand that Cabbarus, not the monarchy, is to blame for the injustices, the punishments, indeed the whole sorry state of the kingdom. I hope to find those who will rally to your side against him."

"You expect much from commoners," said the queen.

"I do," said Torrens. He smiled. "Being one of them myself."

It was close to midnight when Dr. Torrens finished his preparations and the hired wagon arrived to carry his baggage to the port. He traveled ahead in an open coach with all lamps lit, loudly declaring that he wished to be driven to the waterfront. He kept only the small bag with him. He had resigned himself to sacrificing his other belongings.

At the quayside, he entered a seafarer's inn where his inquiries had been received. There he met the master of an outward-bound merchantman and struck a bargain with him to be taken on as a passenger. He paid openly in gold and requested the captain to have his luggage immediately stowed on board. He asked

about the tides, the hour the vessel would sail, and the
length of the voyage. He demanded assurance that his
cabin would be comfortable. He did not say he had
no intention of occupying it.

This business concluded within earshot of all the
company, Dr. Torrens settled himself at a table and
called for a bottle of wine. He drank hardly a glass
before telling his host that he would return momentar-
ily and to keep an eye on the bottle, which he would
attend to when he came back.

He left the inn and strode briskly along the docks.
By now he had singled out the spy he knew Cabbarus
would send: a seaman in canvas slops and a grimy
jacket. The man was dressed as roughly as any common sailor; he was, however, the only one in the room
without dirt or tar under his fingernails.

The doctor's plan was not to avoid the eyes of the
chief minister's agent but, on the contrary, to make
sure the man saw him. The fellow, of course, would
keep him under scrutiny until Torrens was aboard.
Just before setting foot on the gangplank, Torrens
would make a show of having forgotten his bottle at
the inn. He would turn, go back, then suddenly lose
himself in one of the alleyways. With luck, he would
have a few moments head start before his observer
realized he had vanished. Torrens calculated in advance the most suitable unlit alley.

The sailor was following too closely. The man was
incompetent if he thought to go unnoticed. It was all
Torrens could do to pretend not to see him. The man
was at his heels. Torrens halted, reckoning no other
course but to confront him. The man held a knife.
Torrens, too late, realized he had done what he had
never done in his medical practice. He had overlooked
the obvious. He expected a spy. He had not counted
on an assassin.

10

They reached Felden by midafternoon. Las Bombas judged the town would suit them perfectly.

"It's big enough," he said as they halted in the market square, "to have gentry with money in their pockets, and small enough so they won't be too critical. An excellent place for the Oracle Priestess to learn the business. Then, on to greater fame and fortune."

Las Bombas had pinned a number of royal honors and medals to his uniform, unidentifiable but unmistakably noble. Thus decked out, he strode into the largest lodging house and demanded the best suite of furnished apartments. The landlord, too dazzled and flattered to dare bring up the question of advance payment, hurried to show the count the most elegant he could offer. The rooms, on the second floor, had been occupied by a dancing master. The main salon, spacious and high-ceilinged, attracted Las Bombas immediately. He hired the apartments then and there.

Seeing Friska comfortably stabled, the count and Musket went off to survey the town and post the signboard where it would best catch the public eye. Theo,

having unpacked the count's gear, was left to his own
devices. He had never set foot in such luxurious quarters; nor, he was sure, had Mickle. But the girl only
glanced at the ornaments, remarking that Hanno
would have found little worth stealing.

As if that settled the matter, she lost interest in ex-
ploring and flung herself onto the sofa, her legs out-
stretched, feet on an end table. Before entering Felden,
Theo had persuaded her to make at least a token effort at washing at a streamside. Las Bombas had
given her the Trebizonian costume, which suited her
scarcely better than it had suited Theo.

The girl had barely spoken to him since leaving
Born. Why he found this both painful and aggravat-
ing, he did not know. To pass the time, he rummaged
in the count's oddments and found clean paper and a
charcoal stick. He went to the casement, thinking to
sketch the marketplace for his own amusement. His
attention wandered. His eyes returned continually to
Mickle. He began what he expected to be a quick portrait of her. Though he had learned to draw as easily
as he lettered, the closer he studied Mickle the more
difficult she became. He tore up the paper and
started again.

Mickle spoiled his new attempt by jumping up.
Whatever had caused her to ignore him, her curiosity
got the better of her.

"Is that supposed to be me?" She peered over his
shoulder and made a face.

"Supposed to be. But it isn't." Theo felt he was
blushing, but there was nothing he could do about it.
"I can't make you pretty—"

Mickle tossed her head. "Didn't ask you to."

"No, I mean it's more than that. One minute, you
look like a scared little bird, and the next as if you
could stand up to Cabbarus himself. You say you
didn't cry when your friend got hanged, but you cry

in your sleep and don't remember it. Sometimes you look as though butter wouldn't melt in your mouth; then you swear like a dragoon, smoke like a chimney— The count called you a genius, and you can't read or write. I can't catch all that on paper. I don't know what you are."

"That's all right." Mickle grinned at last. "I don't know what you are, either. The count's a rascal, that's plain as a pikestaff. Thumbling's a good fellow. But I don't see how you came to take up with them."

Theo hesitated. He felt a sudden urge to tell the girl what had happened to him and an equal unwillingness to admit anything at all. Before he could decide which to follow, the provisioner's errand boy hauled in a huge basket of food; in another moment, the wine merchant entered with an armload of bottles; and finally Las Bombas himself leading a brigade of tailors, barbers, dressmakers, and carpenters.

Before he understood what was happening, Theo had bolts of cloth draped over his shoulders, and he was being measured, chalked, pinned, and fitted for waistcoats, jackets, and breeches. Mickle had vanished in clouds of lace and billows of satin. Of Musket he saw nothing; only the dwarf's bellowing rose above the din, ordering the carpenters about their work.

"How did you manage all this?" the astonished Theo asked Las Bombas, who was in the hands of two barbers trying to shave and powder him. "How did you pay?"

"By a miracle, my boy." The count beamed. "The miracle of credit. The more we manage to owe these fellows, the better they'll look after us."

By nightfall, when the carpenters had left after nailing up a platform and wooden frame at the end of the salon, the landlord and his wife arrived to serve an enormous supper. Las Bombas interrupted each course to drink a toast to their good fortune, present and future. Theo, overstuffed and exhausted, was glad at last to find his way to the luxury of his own bed in his own chamber. Mickle stayed at the table, making certain nothing remained on the plates.

Too tired even to enjoy the feather pillows and mattress, Theo sank into them like a stone. He had been asleep, he did not know how long, when a scream ripped apart his slumber.

He sat up, head spinning. His body answered before he could gather his wits. By the time he realized the sound had come from Mickle's room, he was on his feet and plunging through the connecting door.

A candle guttered on the night table. Mickle crouched amid a heap of bedclothes. Her face was dead white, streaked with sweat, her eyes wide and staring, empty of everything but terror. He was not sure she even recognized him. He ran to her.

She threw her arms around him. He rocked her back and forth like a child, smoothing her tangled hair. Her cheeks and forehead were icy.

"Nothing, it's nothing," he said. "You had another bad dream. It's gone."

"I was drowning. Water over my head. I kept sinking. I couldn't breathe."

Theo was only now aware that Las Bombas and Musket had been standing behind him. The count, nightcap askew, ordered the dwarf to fetch a glass of wine, then peered anxiously at the girl.

"You'll be fine in a moment. A nightmare, eh? Too much supper, I shouldn't wonder." He sat down beside her and laughed good-naturedly, though giving Theo a quick glance of concern. "Drowning, you say? In that case, you're perfectly safe. No one, to my knowledge, has ever drowned in bed."

Mickle sipped the wine Musket brought. She snuffled and wiped her nose on the back of her hand.

Some color had come back to her cheeks. She smiled at last. After a few more moments, she was making impudent remarks about the count's nightcap, joking with Musket, and mimicking Theo.

Even so, when Las Bombas and Musket went back to their chambers, Theo sensed she was still frightened and stayed, waiting until she fell asleep. He sat watchful the rest of the night. Mickle did not stir.

Next morning, she was quiet and polite, which worried Theo all the more. Musket was busy stringing together the false arms and legs. Las Bombas had gone to hire more chairs for the salon. To distract her and put her in better spirits, Theo started her portrait again.

This time, he had her sit by the casement and ordered her not to move. He worked rapidly at first, with somewhat better result. Then he found himself looking at her so intently that his charcoal stayed poised above the paper as if he had forgotten what he was doing.

Mickle began fidgeting. She complained of a stiff neck and refused to pose longer. She brightened when he offered to go on with her lessons. They sat heads together in a sunny corner while Theo quickly went over the whole alphabet. He planned to go back and teach her a few letters at a time. But when he started his review, Mickle rattled off all twenty-six in nearly perfect order.

"That's all there is to it?"

"I told you it was easy." Theo did not add that he never expected her to do so well so fast. He would gladly have taken credit to himself as schoolmaster. He knew it was not the case. It was not his doing. The girl astonished him. Las Bombas, he thought, had been right. She was a genius. "Next, you'll start making words."

Mickle had lost interest. She looked out the window, turned back, restless.

Finally, she said to him, after much hesitation, "Do you think—about last night, does it mean someday I'm going to drown? The girls in the home used to say that dreams told what was going to happen to you."

"That's nonsense. You had a bad dream, that's all. It's gone, it won't come back."

"It—it's never gone," Mickle burst out. "I've always had it. Not the same every time. Sometimes there's a well and I'm trying to get a drink. Or there's a ditch full of water, but the sides are so high I can't climb out. But it always ends the same: I'm drowning and there's nobody to help.

"Last night, there was a voice, someone saying terrible things. I can't remember what they were. And somebody was laughing. It's the first I ever dreamed that. It was the worst of all."

Theo frowned. "That's what you always dream about?"

"No." The girl had taken his hand, gripping it tightly. "There's another dream I have. It doesn't frighten me. It only makes me want to cry. I dream about my mother and father. It's a nice dream at first. We're happy, laughing, playing hide-and-seek the way we used to do. Then it's my turn to hide and they can't find me. They're calling for me but when I answer they can't hear me. They're very sad and so am I. Because I know I'll never see them again."

She was trembling. After a moment, she pulled away and without another word went to her room.

Theo stood, about to follow. Musket was bellowing for him to come and lend a hand. Something in the girl's account puzzled him. He was sure, outside Born, Mickle had told him her parents were long dead, that she had never known them.

11

The phrenological head was now a working ghost. Swathed in white gauze and attached to the false arms and legs, it appeared a startling spectral figure. Theo and Musket had rigged pulleys from the ceiling, and fixed thin black cords to the mannequin. From their hiding place behind a black screen, they could hoist the figure and make it seem to float across the salon. Las Bombas, meanwhile, instructed Mickle in her role as Oracle Priestess. Before the end of the week, the count was satisfied with all preparations and, that night, flung open his doors to the public.

Theo privately doubted there would be any audience. No one, he believed, would be taken in by such hoaxing. Squinting through a peephole in the screen, he could not believe his eyes. The room was too dim for him to be certain of the number, but most of the chairs were filled. Mickle, robed in black, sat in the light of a single candle, as Theo had suggested. At her signal, he and Musket tugged away at the cords. The ghost obediently rose into the air. The audience gasped; there were a few screams of delicious terror.

Someone in the back of the salon paid Theo's handiwork the compliment of fainting dead away.

Las Bombas urged the company to consult the spirit on any matter of concern. Theo braced himself for disaster as questions showered on the Oracle from all sides. One gentleman demanded to know where his late uncle had hidden his will, as he expected to inherit all the estate. A lady anxiously sought spiritual advice on what colors would be coming into fashion. He expected Mickle to burst out laughing, but the girl kept a straight face. Sitting motionless, eyes closed, she gave every sign of being lost in the deepest trance; with a trick of her voice, she made the phrenological head seem to speak in eerie, sepulchral tones. The answers, however, were so vague that the questioners could take any meaning they chose.

Instead of indignant outcries at being cheated, the audience clamored for more. Las Bombas finally had to declare that the Oracle Priestess was too fatigued; the ghost was dismissed to rejoin its fellow shades. Advising the spectators to come back another day, Las Bombas hustled them out as quickly as possible and locked the doors behind them.

"Magnificent!" cried the count as Theo and Musket came from their hiding place. He threw his arms around Mickle. "Dear girl, you were superb!"

Las Bombas delved into his bulging pockets and tossed handfuls of coins into the air. "Look at this! So much that I lost count of it!"

"No matter how you add it up," muttered Theo, "it still comes to a fraud."

"Indeed it does, my boy," Las Bombas happily answered. "The best I've struck on. Credit where it's due, I have you to thank. You thought of it, you put me onto it. A brilliant notion, and it's all yours."

Theo said nothing in reply. He was ashamed of himself, appalled that his scheme had worked so well. He also had to admit that he was not entirely displeased.

Mickle seemed to have no qualms whatever. During the days following, she was in the best of spirits. The nightmare had not come back, nor had the other dream. Since the Oracle Priestess had no duties until evening, the rest of the time was her own. Mornings she spent with Theo going over the alphabet. She knew her letters perfectly and had begun writing them as quickly as she had learned to say them.

Mickle kept her part of the bargain. Afternoons were her turn to play schoolmistress and teach her sign language to Theo. He did not learn as quickly as his former pupil.

"No, no, you've got it all wrong again," Mickle told him. "Move your thumb up, not sideways. Here, watch my fingers."

Little by little, he caught the knack. He practiced with her at every opportunity, adding improvements. Now that Mickle could spell, he devised a finger motion for each letter. Thus, when Mickle's gestures did not exactly suit the circumstances, she spelled out words of explanation. Within little more than a week, they could signal anything they pleased, so quickly that no outsider could guess they were using a silent code. Though Las Bombas and Musket could not fail to notice the two young people passed most of their time in each other's company, they did not comment.

For the rest, Theo expected, even hoped, the novelty of The Oracle Priestess would wear off. The Feldeners, instead, crowded the salon each night in growing numbers. Las Bombas crowed over the receipts. Theo's conscience smarted like a skinned knee.

He finally asked the count when they would move on.

Las Bombas blinked at him. "What an idea! We've barely skimmed the cream. In fact, I'm thinking of doubling the admission price."

"I'm thinking we should stop altogether," blurted Theo. "I've gone along this far, which I shouldn't have done. There must be something better than cheating people."

"Who's cheating anyone?" protested the count. "Harmless amusement! Do you think for a moment they believe one bit of it? Are they complaining? Set your mind at rest, my boy. Now, here's a thought for you. Suppose we put up refreshment tables in the hall. That would be a new attraction."

Next night, Theo was almost willing to admit the count was right. The Oracle Priestess had become fashionable among the Felden gentry, probably through lack of better diversion. The audience, more and more, came to see and be seen; to be amused by the antics of the phrenological head; to admire the wistful charms of the Priestess. There was much gossip and laughter; no one, as far as Theo could gather, truly believed in the girl's ghostly pronouncements. Las Bombas might as well have opened a comedy theater.

However, among the spectators who used the occasion to put on all their finery, Theo glimpsed a man and woman dressed in deep mourning. Their garb alone would have set them apart. From the woman's raw hands, the man's weathered face and heavy shoulders, Theo guessed the couple to be smallholders or tenant farmers. The two sat ill at ease amid the town dwellers.

Only toward the end of the evening did the woman venture to stand. She made an awkward curtsy to Mickle and to the phrenological head, causing a few titters among the audience. She glanced around uncomfortably and looked ready to sit down again without a word.

"Come, madam," said Las Bombas, "the Priestess grows fatigued. If you wish to consult the spirit, come out with it."

"Sir"—the woman hesitated, reddening—"our girl's dead a week now. It was the fever, you see. We can't have her back, I know that. All I want to ask, can you tell us: Wherever she is, is she happy there?"

The phrenological head assured its questioner that the girl was happier than she had ever been in all her life. The woman stammered her gratitude for setting their hearts at rest.

Las Bombas then asked for more questions. None came. The audience had turned restless and embarrassed; some stood up to leave, as if the woman's grief had cast a shadow over their entertainment. The count finally declared the séance ended.

"How can you do it?" Theo demanded, as soon as the last of the spectators had gone. "They were heartbroken, those two. It wasn't just foolishness for them. They took it seriously. We told them a pack of lies."

"My boy, they were quite satisfied," answered Las Bombas. "What do you want?"

"No more of it," said Theo, "that's what I want. Call it harmless amusement if you like. You're taking advantage of people who don't know any better. It's dishonest, it's contemptible." He rounded on Mickle. "You understand what I mean, don't you? You see what we're doing."

"I'm doing what you wanted," the girl retorted. "It was your idea in the first place, wasn't it?"

"No, you don't understand, either," burst out Theo. "Can't you even see what's right or wrong? Or don't you care? I shouldn't have expected any better from you."

Mickle gasped as if he had slapped her in the face. Instead of answering, she pulled the hood over her head and ran to her chamber.

Theo could have bitten his tongue as soon as he had spoken the words. He started after her. Las Bombas held him back.

"Let be. You've hurt the child's feelings already, and you'll make matters worse, the state you're in. Patch it up in the morning."

"Let's leave here," said Theo. "There must be something else we can do."

"Change The Oracle Priestess? When it's working so marvelously? Ridiculous! Out of the question! Have a good sleep. You'll feel better tomorrow."

Without replying, Theo went to his room and flung himself on the bed. Tormented at wounding Mickle, he only hoped he could make it up to her. That still did not satisfy his conscience. Las Bombas had no intention of changing his ways. He was fond of the count, as fond as he had ever been of Anton. But the man was a born rogue, and Theo was well on the road to becoming one himself. Anton would not have been proud of him. The answer was clear. He had gone far enough, perhaps too far. To save whatever shreds of honesty were left him, he would have to quit Las Bombas, the sooner the better. Now, he told himself, this very night. If he waited, he feared he would not have the strength to do it.

No sooner had he made up his mind to that than he realized he could not leave Mickle. The idea was unbearable to him. Much as he had hurt the girl, he believed he could finally make her understand. She would come with him, if he tried his best to persuade her.

He stood and went quickly to her room. He raised his hand to tap on the door, but the motion froze in midair. To his dismay, he realized he had forgotten one thing. He was a wanted criminal, a fugitive who could be arrested at any moment. He did not dare ask her to stay with him. Even if she wanted to, he could not let her. She would be as much at risk as himself. She would be safe with Las Bombas, mountebank though he was.

He let his hand fall to his side. He stood, uncertain, at the door. Finally he turned away. The portrait, unfinished, lay on a table. He was about to pick it up. He shook his head. It would pain him less if he had no reminder of her.

He carried nothing with him as he went quietly down the stairs. He could not trust himself to say farewell. He strode across the market square. The town slept. Though nearly summer, the night was cool.

There was no question in Theo's mind. He had done the right and honorable thing. For the first time since taking up with Las Bombas, his conscience was at ease.

And he felt miserable.

PART THREE
Florian's Children

12

The lodging house at the end of Strawmarket Street stood as one of the marvels of Freyborg: the marvel being that it stood at all. The spider webs in every corner appeared to be its strongest support. The narrow staircase lurched up three flights and stayed in place out of habit. Mold flowered from cracks in the walls. The roof shed its tiles like autumn leaves. The lodgings, nevertheless, had two things to recommend them: cheap rent and a landlord who never asked questions.

The topmost room was a little bigger than a baker's oven. In summer, the stifling tenant could take comfort knowing that he would, in due season, freeze. This cubbyhole was often vacant. For the past two months, however, it had been occupied by a public letter writer calling himself De Roth.

His new name had been Theo's choice. His new occupation and living quarters he owed to Florian.

On the night he had left Felden, he struck out across country, heading generally south. He trudged without a halt until daybreak. Even then he did not stop until some hours later when his legs gave out. He

had made up his mind not to think of Mickle, the
count, Musket, or anything connected with them. In
consequence, he thought of nothing else. Mickle's ab-
sence crept over him like a toothache: at first ignored,
then denied, then taking command altogether.

He kept on a straight path for the next few days.
He slept in barns or hayricks, if one happened to be in
his way. Otherwise, he crawled under bushes or flung
himself down in open fields. He neither asked for nor
refused hospitality from the farm folk. Sometimes he
mucked out stables or chopped logs for a sack of food.
Convinced that he had acted honorably, he was proud
of his strength of will. He also caught a cold.

He limped into Freyborg around midday, bursting
with lofty sentiments and a stopped-up nose. Perhaps
he had intended going there from the first. In the
days before Cabbarus, when Anton worked for the
university scholars, the ancient town had come to be a
sparkling, almost magical, fountainhead of learning
for Theo. He found it gray, the streets narrow, the famous university tower smaller than he had imagined.
He was too hungry to think of being disappointed.

There was a tavern on the near side of the square,
facing a statue of Augustine the Great. He went inside, hoping to trade work for a meal. In the busy
room, he saw no one who might be the host. The waiters ignored him. He squeezed onto the end of a bench
and leaned his head against the wall.

His tablemates, half a dozen young men and
women, were talking and laughing. What drew Theo's
attention was the bowl of soup in front of his neigh-
bor, a massive-browed, bullnecked youth whose hair
had already begun thinning. Theo's nose was not too
blocked to keep out the aroma, and he lost himself in
it.

"Stock," said the young man directly across from

Theo, "this gentleman appears to be memorizing your soup."

Theo started, realizing his head had come forward little by little as if the bowl were a magnet. He stammered an apology, which only brought him under scrutiny of all the party.

"What has now to be determined," the speaker went on, as attentive silence fell over the table, "is the reason for such fascination. Is it the essential nature of the soup, hidden from all of us? Stock's table manners, hidden from none of us? Or still another cause?"

Though only a few years older than Theo, the speaker seemed to have crossed some invisible line giving him an authority beyond the number of his birthdays. His hair was light brown and he wore it long and loose. Pockmarks sprayed his cheeks and the bridge of his finely drawn nose. He was studying Theo with apparently idle amusement; but his gray eyes took in everything at once, observing, calculating, and summing up the result.

Theo sensed he was being laughed at or soon would be. Had he looked in a mirror these past days he would have seen good reason for it. His hair was matted, his clothes wrinkled and muddy, his face dirty and wind-raw.

"He's hungry, Florian," put in one of the young women, fair-haired and broad-faced, with the swollen hands of a laundress.

"Obviously. But to what degree? Is he hungry enough to risk Master Jellinek's concoction? This remains to be seen, theory proved in practice. Pass him your bowl, Stock. Go on, don't be a pig about it."

Chuckling and grumbling at the same time, Stock did as he was asked. Florian raised a finger and two waiters arrived instantly. One set a goblet in front of Theo, the other poured wine into it.

Florian lifted his own glass. "To the health of one who is ever in our thoughts: our chief minister."

Theo reddened. He was too tired to be polite. He pushed away the glass. "Drink to him yourself. I won't."

"My children!" cried Florian. "Do you hear? This youngster, clearly perishing from hunger, stands nevertheless on his principles. He sets us an example. Put to the same test, would we do as well?" He turned to Theo. "Spoken bravely but carelessly. You haven't the mind of a lawyer, which is a great blessing for you. Otherwise, you would have observed the health was not specified as 'good.' You jumped to a conclusion. In this case, a wrong one. Would you care to reconsider?

"Seize the opportunity," Florian continued. "Don't think we banquet like this every day. We are celebrating the anniversary of Rina's birth." He nodded at the laundress, who rose and made a mocking curtsy. "With us, it is feast or famine, more often the latter."

Theo ventured to ask if they were students. Hoots and whistles followed his question.

"We forgive your unintended offense," Florian said. "No one with a thirst for knowledge goes to the university now. Half the faculty has resigned, the other half gives courses in advanced ignorance. The Royal Grant is no longer very royal nor much granted. Public intelligence, in the view of Cabbarus, is a public nuisance, like a stray cat. If unfed, it will go away. But allow me to present my children, my fledgling eagles waiting impatiently to spread their wings.

"Our worthy Stock, though he may look like a prize bull, is by inclination a poet; by temperament, a dreamer. This one, Justin"—he pointed to a thin, pale youth, close to Theo's age, with hair so yellow it shone almost white, and with long-lashed eyes of astonishing violet—"Justin has the face of an angel; whereas, in fact, he is a bloodthirsty sort of devil. The result, possibly, of seeing his father hanged. Our two goddesses, the golden Rina and the russet Zara, guide and inspire us."

Florian stood, laid a hand on his bosom, and struck an exaggerated oratorical pose. "As for me, I pursued the study of law until I learned there is only one: the decree of Nature herself that men are brothers; and the only criminals, those who break her statute. Students? Yes. But our classroom is the world."

When his companions, playing audience, finished cheering and pounding the table, Florian went on more quietly.

"And you, youngster? What brings you here? Your trade appears to be professional scarecrow. You may find little call for your services."

Theo's fever was singing lightly in his ears. The food and drink had turned him a little giddy. Florian, on top of that, seemed to have the odd power of drawing him out. Though he kept enough caution to say nothing of Dorning, Theo hardly stopped talking long enough to catch his breath. He gladly unburdened himself, having spoken no more than a dozen words in a dozen days. He detailed his journey with Las Bombas and tried to explain that he had left Mickle for her own good. He finally realized he had been babbling and let his account trail off.

"He loved her," sighed Rina. "It was noble of him. It was beautiful."

"It was stupid," said Zara.

Florian raised a hand. "Children, we are not called upon to render a verdict, only to ponder what should be done."

He spoke apart with the auburn-haired Zara for a moment, and turned back to Theo. "The russet divinity will see you housed for the time being, Master—would you care to tell us your name?"

"It's"—Theo paused, remembering the order for his arrest, and hoping to cover his tracks as best he could—"it's—De Roth."

"Go along with her, then, Master De Roth." Florian grinned. "Here, we feed our stray cats."

Zara led him to Strawmarket Street. The girl said little, as did Theo, still rankling at her comment. When he told her he had no money for rent, Zara shrugged. He could, she advised, settle it with the landlord some other time. Florian, meanwhile, would vouch for him.

"What does Florian do?" Theo asked. "What's his work?"

"His work?" Zara gave him a hard smile. "He works at being Florian."

13

Next day, having slept the clock around, Theo found his way back to the tavern. He wanted to thank Florian and take leave of him. He saw none of the company in the public room. Jellinek, a stout little man, surprisingly good-natured for a landlord, recognized Theo. He motioned with his thumb toward a cubicle beside the kitchen. Because of the commotion behind the door, Theo's knock went unheard or ignored. He let himself in, though uneasy at intruding on what sounded like a furious oration.

It was Stock and, as Theo would learn, only his way of holding forth on any subject. The burly poet stalked back and forth, arms waving. Florian, Justin, and several others unknown to Theo sat around a plank table.

"A battle, I say, is a poem," Stock was declaiming. "A sonnet of death, men for verses, blood for punctuation. Attack and counterattack, rhyme against rhyme, cavalry against foot—"

"How do you reckon artillery, then?" broke in one of the listeners, called, as Theo later found out, Luther. "The exclamation marks? Clever notion. It only has one flaw. It has nothing to do with real fighting. Take my advice, keep to scribbling."

Glimpsing Theo, Florian beckoned. "Stock has given up being a field marshal of poetry in favor of being a poetic field marshal. And what are you up to?"

"I'll have to move on. I'll try to send you money for my lodging."

"Going, are you? Where?"

"It doesn't matter. Wherever I can find some sort of work."

"These aren't the best days to go wandering around the country," said Florian.

"I need to make a living, one way or another."

Florian thought for a while. "Do you write a clear hand? There's room for a public letter writer here in Freyborg. The previous incumbent is no longer with us, and Stock finds the profession demeaning to his genius."

"Yes, I could do that," Theo began eagerly. He stopped short. The day before, he had said nothing of what had happened in Dorning. He was still reluctant to do so. If Florian knew the truth about him, he might well withdraw his offer. Harboring a fugitive was as much a crime as being one. He took a breath and hurried on. "You may not want me to stay. There's something I have to tell you."

"Go at it, then." Seeing his discomfort, Florian motioned for the others to leave.

"What you ought to know," said Theo, once they were alone, "is—I'm in some trouble."

"We all are. Go on."

After his first painful hesitation, Theo poured out the whole account. His surprise, when he finished, was Florian's lack of surprise.

"Youngster, I'm sorry," said Florian. "A brutal business, but I've heard far worse."

"If I stay here, it could put you in trouble. And your friends, too."

"Don't worry, we can manage it," said Florian. "In fact, you couldn't be in a safer place. So, it's settled."

"One more thing."

"Oh? You seem to have quite a lot on your mind."

"My name. It isn't De Roth."

Florian laughed. "We have something in common. My name isn't Florian."

From then on, a bench and table were reserved for Theo in Jellinek's tavern, with pen, ink, and paper suppled by the host until he earned enough to buy his own. It had all been arranged so quickly, as if Florian needed only to snap his fingers. With Florian, he came to know, this was how things happened.

In the following days, as he became a familiar sight in his corner, he drew a small but steady stream of customers.

Some were able to write slowly and painfully, others not at all. None could draft a letter setting out what they had in mind to say. The task of Theo was to sort their ideas and try to put them on paper.

An old woman needed an appeal to the Royal Prosecutor on behalf of her son, in prison for a crime he did not commit. A kitchen maid expecting a child wished to write her sweetheart, who had gone off to Marianstat, and lie to him that all went well with her. There were letters swearing undying love; letters begging for it; furious letters threatening lawsuits; timid letters asking more time to pay a debt. To the public letter writer, as much a piece of furniture as the bench he sat on, none hesitated to pour out every sorrow, shame, fear, and hope. Most of the letters went unanswered.

Nights, Theo often lay awake tossing and sweating on his pallet in the loft, chewing over his clients' misfortunes as if he had to absorb them before he could rest. Sometimes, on the contrary, he could not go to sleep fast enough to escape them. He was overwhelmed, appalled. Finally, he grew modest. Until then, he had believed he suffered a very high quality of misery. It took him a little time to accept the humbling idea that most of his customers were in worse case than himself.

Mornings, he went to Jellinek's tavern. Florian was sometimes there, sometimes not. He had the habit of disappearing for several days on end. When he reappeared, something in his bearing warned Theo against asking him where he had been.

Stock and the others were used to these absences and did not comment on them. Theo, again, sensed that he should not raise questions. Otherwise, he got on well with them and enjoyed their company.

The golden divinity and the russet divinity, he soon realized, were clearly in love with Florian: the former, dreamily and happily; the latter, bitterly and almost against her will. Stock, who usually turned furious at the least criticism of his poetry, listened closely to Florian's opinions. For the most part, Florian kept a wry good humor. Sometimes, however, his remarks could sting. The others were able to shrug them off, but on one occasion when Florian made a mildly sarcastic remark to Justin, the latter nearly burst into tears.

"You should have answered back," Theo later told him. "You shouldn't have let him hurt your feelings."

Justin turned his eyes on Theo. "If he asked me to, I'd die for him."

To be called "my child" by Florian was a title of honor. It had not been granted to Theo. Nevertheless, he yearned for it. Despite Florian's help and interest, Theo was aware of a certain lack of acceptance. Perhaps he had not yet earned it, perhaps he did not deserve it. In the lives of Florian and his children, some part was held back from him, and he was puzzled by it.

What also puzzled Theo was how Florian stayed out of prison, for the man spoke his mind whenever and wherever he chose. The townsfolk worshiped him, and Theo first believed the officers feared a riot if they laid hands on him. Theo was wrong, as he learned one afternoon when two constables strode into the tavern and began badgering Jellinek for information about a runaway apprentice.

Theo broke into a sweat, sure it was himself they were asking about. Jellinek, sweating as much as Theo, kept wiping his hands and face with his apron. Florian finally got up from his usual seat.

He sauntered over to the constables. Smiling, he quietly suggested they leave. He did not raise hand or voice. The smile never left his face, but his gray eyes had turned bright and hard as ice. The officers blustered a few moments, then declared the matter unimportant and hurried out. Theo understood. It was not the townsfolk they feared. It was Florian.

Florian's assurance of safety had not been idle boasting, and Theo was grateful. His spirits had begun mending a little. At times, however, he turned restless, feeling his days were without sense or point.

"I'm glad for the work," he told Florian one morning in the tavern, "but none of it does much good. I write their letters, but nothing comes of it. I'm not making anything better for them. What's the use?"

"The use," answered Florian, "is that they need you. There's always a chance something may work out. You give them a grain of hope, at least. Be satisfied you can do anything at all.

"As a matter of fact," he went on, "I might have something else for you. I warn you, it won't be easy."

"What is it?"

"We'll talk about it when the times comes."

Theo, excited, pressed him for some hint, but Florian left, saying no more. The old woman whose son was in prison had been waiting patiently. Theo had written her same letter to the Royal Prosecutor so often that he knew it word for word. He had, until then, considered that the best service he could do would be to tell her to go away, that it was a lost cause. He beckoned to her.

"Come along, mother," he said. "Let's try again."

14

"There's a dead one." The boy held up his lantern and leaned over the side of the rowboat. "Pull hard, Sparrow."

The girl did as her brother asked. The craft bobbed alongside the stone steps leading from the embankment to the dock. The boy, Weasel, was small and as thin as his namesake. Sparrrow, a few years older and the stronger, took charge of the rowing on their nightly ventures into the port.

The man lay on his belly, half in, half out of the water. His legs swung gently in the tide.

Sparrow shipped her oars. "Drowned, is he?"

Weasel threw a line around the iron stanchion and hopped out of the boat. He squatted by the body but could not turn it. Sparrow came to help. They saw the knife hilt.

"A brawl." Weasel nodded his head in solemn professional judgment. He tugged until the weapon came free of the breast. "It's a good blade."

He put the knife in his belt. Sparrow had been deftly going through the pockets. She had no fear of

the dead. On the other hand, she was terrified of spi-
ders.

The jacket and canvas slops yielded nothing. She
made a face and shrugged her shoulders. The lantern
light showed a bulky form a few steps higher. Sparrow got to her feet. The boy, too, noticed the figure
and clambered after his sister.

"I knew it was a brawl," Weasel declared with satisfaction.

This man was white-haired and blunt-featured. One
sleeve, bloodsoaked, had been slashed up the arm.
The girl rummaged in the pockets. This time she
whistled. She had discovered a purse of coins, and
something else: The man was alive. Weasel crouched
beside her, greatly interested. They had never found a
live one.

"What shall we do with him, Sparrow?"

The girl chewed her lower lip. She was a sharp-
faced creature, more vixen than bird. The man was
looking at her, muttering something she could not
make out.

She bent closer, listening, then glanced at Weasel. "I
don't know what he's saying, but I don't think he
wants to stay here."

"I shouldn't wonder," said Weasel.

Like her brother, Sparrow wore a garment of sack-
ing. Her one vanity was the kerchief about her head.
She undid it and awkwardly bound up the man's arm.
Her patient groaned and made a feeble gesture.

"What's he after?" Until then, Weasel had given all
his attention to the unusual find. Now, at the edge of
the circle of light, he glimpsed a leather case. He scut-
tled over and picked it up. "This?"

Weasel snapped open the catch and peered inside.
"Knives and things. They'll be worth something."

Sparrow had finished her work and had come to
her decision. "We'll keep him."

"What will Keller say?"

"He'll be glad. It's company for him, isn't it?"

The two set about hauling the man down the steps and aboard the boat. He was conscious enough to make some small effort to help. Otherwise, his salvagers would have had to leave their prize where they found it. Weasel cast off the line. Sparrow labored to get the craft under way before the tide turned against her.

The River Vespera flowed through Marianstat. Near the port, narrow spits of land reached out from the banks: The Fingers. Part marsh, part scrub lining a maze of inlets, The Fingers formed a hand grasping whatever floated by. Human bodies, as well as animal carcasses, sometimes came to bob among the reeds They were picked over for anything useful and sent on their voyage again by the scavengers who lived and made a living there.

These river and shore dwellers avoided each other. They had their favorite backwaters which they defended jealously, tending and harvesting them like frugal farmers, selling their crop for a pittance in Marianstat. When the harvest was lean, those lucky enough to have a boat explored other waters. The docks usually offered gleanings of some value.

It was toward The Fingers that Sparrow plied her oars, eager to examine her passenger at greater length and leisure. It was nearly full daylight by the time she beached the rowboat. The man, eyes closed, slumped in the stern. The scavengers could not move him.

"Keller!" Sparrow shouted. "Come help."

From a crude hut amid the bushes a little distance from shore, a lanky figure cautiously put out his head, then strode toward the youngsters.

"Hurry," ordered Sparrow. "We brought company for you. He may be dead."

"Marvelous," the man tartly replied. He was youngish, with rumpled chestnut hair and a pale face. "Exactly what I need."

Weasel was pulling him by his coatsleeve. Keller glanced at the man in the stern, then hurried closer, paying no heed to the water sloshing about his knees.

"Come on," said Sparrow. "Give us a hand."

"Water rats," said Keller, with a bemused laugh, "You've caught yourselves a Royal Physician."

Dr. Torrens, opening his eyes, could be certain only of two things: He was alive and his arm hurt. His recollections, otherwise, were dim and confused. He had been hauled off by a pair of goblins. Or he might have dreamed it. Lying on a dirt floor, a stranger bending over him, he had no idea where he was. A ragged girl and boy were staring at him.

"We've been waiting two days for you to wake up," the stranger said. "I can tell you, there were moments when I had my doubts. This is Sparrow and her brother, Weasel. They would have me believe you put a knife in a sailor's ribs. They find that intriguing. They are much impressed by you, Dr. Torrens."

"You know me?" The physician, astonished, managed to sit up.

"By sight and by reputation. You are one of the few who do not employ the services of leeches. Very sensible, since we already have a large one disguised as a chief minister. Ah—forgive me for imposing my opinion on someone too weak to disagree with it."

Torrens grimaced. "I would hardly do so. You recognize me, but I cannot say the same for you."

"You might know me better if I presented myself as Old Kasperl."

In spite of his discomfort, Dr. Torrens laughed in surprise at hearing the name. It was the title of a comic journal circulated throughout Marianstat. "You? Is that possible?"

"Since I pen the words to put in his mouth and, in fact, created him, I suppose I may claim his identity. The Bear's, too."

"Your journal has given me pleasure," said Torrens. "Those talks between Old Kasperl and his bear show a nice wit. But—Old Kasperl? With his peasant jacket, his tankard, his gray whiskers? I would expect his author to be a much older man."

"The times we live in age us rapidly," said Keller. "Even so, I take it as a compliment. I make nonsense of the world to help others make sense of it."

"A remark worthy of Old Kasperl," said Torrens.

"Actually, the Bear is the smarter. He usually sets Old Kasperl straight, as you may have noticed. The chief minister, I am happy to say, finds their humor cuts a little too close to the bone. They were— embodied, that is, in their creator—quite recently invited to a hanging: their own. A tribute to their ability to nettle Cabbarus, but an honor I was grateful to forgo. A whole crew of us scriveners awaited the writing of our last pages in the Carolia Fortress. A few succeeded in escaping. I joined them, not wishing Old Kasperl to make his final public appearance on the gallows. Once out, we all separated. I made my way here. These water rats have been most hospitable. They admire lawbreakers.

"But I weary you, Doctor. Tell me how I may set you on your path, since you are clearly not here by choice. Trust my discretion about the dead sailor."

"I killed him," Torrens answered flatly. "I have not forgiven myself for that. My occupation is to save life, not take it. But he would have taken mine. Unfortunately for him, I know the vulnerabilities of the human body better than he did. He was not a sailor, by the way. Cabbarus had sent him. For you see, I too am under sentence of death."

"Bravo!" cried Keller. "You'll be a hero in the eyes of our generous water rats. In mine, too, for that matter."

Dr. Torrens was grateful he had fallen into the hands of a journalist and two urchins rather than those of another physician. Instead of dosing and cauterizing him, in their ignorance they merely let him rest, fed him as best they could, and kept his wound clean. As a result, he recovered quickly. Keller, following the doctor's instructions, made a sling from a linen garment he found in a pile of rags.

"Sparrow and Weasel will not object to our making free with their rubbish collection," said Keller, adjusting the sling. "Some of it no doubt was here when they arrived: like an ancestral heritage. Good stewards, they have added to it."

"This is not their home, then?"

"It is now. If I understand Sparrow, they found it empty and simply moved in. They have no parents, except in the biological sense. They may stay, they may move on. They are here now, which is all that matters to them."

"It is monstrous to think of them growing up in this—sewer, for it is hardly better than one."

"On the contrary," said Keller, "they are among the lucky. Marianstat swarms with waifs and strays, as you surely know. Sometimes I think they must live in the cracks of the sidewalks. For them, what you call a sewer would be a holiday in the country. We, too, should be glad of it as long as we are obliged to stop here."

"In my case, it cannot be much longer," said Torrens. During his recovery, the court physician and the journalist had come to have confidence in each other. Though gloomier by temperament than Torrens expected from the creator of Old Kasperl, the writer could be comical and scathing in his remarks about Cabbarus. When their two hosts were off on their daily rounds, Torrens revealed his hope of rallying opposition to the chief minister.

"Master Cabbarus hardly lacks admirers," said Keller. "That is, they would admire him most if he were at the end of a rope. They are scattered throughout the kingdom. Which sums up the difficulty. They are scattered."

"Are there no leaders among them? None who can help me?"

"A colleague wrote to me earlier this year," said Keller. "He lives in Belvitsa, some leagues up-country. He mentioned rumors of one individual, something of a firebrand."

"Can you put me in touch with your colleague?"

"I should like to put myself in touch with him. Old Kasperl and the Bear will have to go to ground, as far as possible from Marianstat. The Fingers are delightful in their own peculiar way, but not as a permanent address."

"The roads, of course, will be watched."

"Closely. Except for one. An excellent highway, it may get us clear of the city. From that point, it will be up to us. I say 'us' because I suggest we travel together."

"Agreed," said Torrens. "But this highway?"

"At our door. The Vespera. Since we cannot walk it, we shall have to sail it. Since we have to sail it, we require a boat. As for the boat—"

"Take the children's?" Torrens frowned. "It's their only means of livelihood."

"Although by trade a journalist," said Keller, "I nevertheless decline to rob children. Our water rats might row us beyond the city and put us ashore well upriver. Money, I think, might induce them."

"No doubt," said Torrens, "but my purse is gone."

"Sparrow has it. I saw her with it. Let me convince her to part with it. I shall appeal to her better nature, to her sense of honor, of which she must have some remaining trace."

When Sparrow and Weasel came back, Keller sat down in front of him. "Water rats, I shall ask you a question. Are you thieves?"

"No," piped up Weasel, "but I'd like to be."

"I'm no thief either," said Sparrow. "I never had the luck."

"Even so," Keller went on, "I believe you have a purse of money belonging to this gentleman. In effect, you stole it from him."

"Did not!" cried Sparrow. "It's my pickings. I found it."

"Yes, you found it. In his pocket," said Keller. "Now, pay attention to my reasoning. Had you taken it from a dead man, that would be one thing. Since he was very much alive, that's something else. That is stealing."

"I shan't give it back."

"You shall keep it," Keller agreed, "but under different conditions. This gentleman and I have urgent business upriver. Were you to row us a certain distance, the purse would be quite honorably and honestly yours—to pay our passage and to compensate you for your hospitality. You may not understand the finer points of my logic, but—"

"We'll take you," said Sparrow. "Why didn't you just come straight out and ask?"

"So much for logic." Keller sighed. "So much for honor."

15

Some nights after his hint of new work for Theo, Florian led him to a wine merchant's warehouse near the market square. The merchant himself unbolted the door and motioned them down a flight of steps. In the cellar, behind a wall of vats, a space had been cleared to provide a large, low-ceilinged room. On a trestle table were candles and wooden boxes. Stock was pacing back and forth while Zara and Justin rummaged through the boxes. Rina had just set down a wooden plank.

"My children," declared Florian, "greet your architect and artificer." He bowed to Theo. "Youngster, you are no longer an apprentice, but master."

Theo had no idea what Florian was talking about. His eyes fell on a pile of lumber and odd bits of ironware. It was a press—the fragments, rather, of several presses.

"Cabbarus makes it his business to close print shops," Florian said. "We make it our business to open them. At least one, so far. When the king's officers tear down a press, we salvage a few pieces, like little birds picking up crumbs."

"But—how? How did you manage to bring all this here?"

"That doesn't matter," said Florian. "The question is: Can you put it together?"

"I don't know." Theo was staggered at the work needed. "Each press is a little different. It's not just cobbling one piece to another. I don't know. But, yes, I'll try."

"Do it," said Florian. "If you want anything, you'll have it."

"Like the phoenix!" cried Stock. "Like the legendary bird that rises from its own ashes, this press will rise from its own rubbish heap."

"Leave off," said Zara. "If you mean to work, stay. If not, go to Jellinek's."

The bulky poet seized a sheet of paper from the table. "I shall set to work immediately. I have some verses in mind. They shall be the first offsprings of our mechanical phoenix. The original laid only a single egg, but we can hatch thousands."

"Your verses can wait," said Florian. He glanced at Theo. "When our young friend first came here, he told me something in private. If he agrees, I think now it should be made public. The killing of an innocent man by Royal Officers should not be kept a secret."

Theo, still puzzled, nodded and Florian went on. "I suggest you write an account of your master: why they destroyed his press and, indeed, destroyed him. Set it all down, exactly as it happened. Print it. We'll get it into as many hands as we can. The people of Westmark will have another example of how Cabbarus goes about his business."

Theo agreed willingly. From then on, he worked at three occupations. Days, he sat in the tavern and drafted letters for his customers. Evenings, he labored over the press in the warehouse. Afterwards, far into the night, he tried to write his account.

It was not as easy as he had supposed. Anton had been as much a father as a master to him. He found himself thinking more of his own upbringing than what had happened that night in Dorning. He tried to see Anton through the eyes of a stranger: a provincial tradesman who had seen little of the world beyond his shop, whose life was in the books he printed. He remembered Anton reproaching him for wishing to have Cabbarus by the throat. Yet, the man had fought furiously to defend his press. Trying to define Anton, he tried to define himself. None of it, however, was useful to his pamphlet, and he began all over again.

The press, meanwhile, took shape little by little. He had chosen Zara for his devil. She was sharp-tongued but quick-witted and, by trade a dressmaker, clever with her hands. Rina and Justin sorted the hodgepodge of type: a tedious job but, since it was for Florian, neither complained. Stock did the heavy work, grumbling that he was a poet, not a packmule.

When the press at last was ready—Stock had insisted on naming it The Westmark Phoenix—Florian treated them to a supper at Jellinek's: a double celebration, since Theo had finished his pamphlet and Florian had praised it.

While Stock declaimed verses and Justin nodded over the remnants of the feast, Florian left the table at a signal from Jellinek. Returning shortly, he drew Theo aside and led him to the cubicle next to the kitchen.

Luther was waiting. Of all Florian's friends, he was least seen and least known to Theo. A graying, leathery man older than the others, he could have been a wheelwright, stonemason, or artisan of some sort. His clothes were damp and travel-stained.

"Luther has come up from the south," said Florian, "by way of Nierkeeping. You may be interested in what he can tell you about some friends of yours."

"I've never been to Nierkeeping," said Theo. "I have no friends there."

"I think you do," said Florian. "Your former colleague. Whatever he's calling himself at the moment, Luther's description matches what you told me."

"There was a girl with him," cried Theo. "Mickle—"

"And still is," said Luther. "A half-size fellow, too. They're both in the town lockup."

"Why?" Theo's heart sank as quickly as it had leaped. "What have they done?"

"I don't know," said Luther. "They're better off than the other one. He's in the middle of the market square. Locked in a cage."

"What for?" Theo seized Luther's arm. "What are they doing to him?"

"From what I gather, punishing him for some kind of mischief. He's been caged up for a couple of days. They aren't even feeding him."

"I have to go there. Zara can manage the press."

"When we first met," said Florian, "I recall you seemed delighted to be rid of the fellow."

"He wasn't in trouble then. Mickle's there, too. And Musket. I have to get them out."

"You can't," said Luther. "Nierkeeping's full of troops, for one thing. For another, the town's in an ugly mood. You wouldn't last a minute."

"I can't stay here and do nothing. There must be some way. I'm going. I'll take my chances."

"I won't let you do that," said Florian.

"Won't let me?" cried Theo. "No one's going to stop me. Not even you."

Theo was astonished at his own words. No one spoke that way to Florian. Nevertheless, he stood his ground and looked him squarely in the face.

Florian half smiled. "You're more a hothead than I supposed. No, I won't let you. That's to say I won't let you go alone."

"You'll help me, then?"

Florian's gray eyes had a light in them. "As I think of it, a visit to Nierkeeping might suit all of us very well. We could profit from a breath of country air." He glanced at Luther.

"It could be profitable, as I was telling you," replied the artisan. "Large risk, but large gain."

"We'll do it," said Florian. He turned to Theo. "But I'm afraid we can't leave immediately."

"When? How soon?"

Florian grinned. "Within the hour. Would that stretch your patience beyond bearing?"

"I'm in your debt," said Theo. "I'll make it up to you. I give you my word."

"Accepted and valued," said Florian. "Go and tell the others."

16

Theo huddled under the straw in the back of the wagon. The moon was down, the sky beginning to pale. Justin, beside him, was curled up and sleeping soundly. In front, Florian held the reins lightly, allowing the horse to make its own pace. Zara, dressed as a peasant woman, drowsed with her head on his shoulder. She had insisted on going with them, so Rina, under protest, had stayed in Freyborg: to keep an eye on the press and await any urgent word from Florian. Stock and Luther had ridden ahead on fresh mounts. Theo marveled that Florian had set all in train so quickly. It was, he understood, part of the business of being Florian. He was grateful.

He had tried to thank Florian, who shrugged it aside as if the journey were, in fact, only a jaunt through the countryside. For a while, so it appeared. The wagon rattled along dirt roads with flat, stubble fields on either side. Morning, when it came, was bright and crisp. There was an air of holiday, with Florian in the best of spirits.

They reached a paved road and, later, a fingerpost pointing toward Nierkeeping. Instead of following it,

Florian turned off and drove into the woodlands covering the swelling hills.

When Theo ventured to ask why, Florian only replied, "Leave that to me. For the moment, all you need to do is enjoy the view. It's one of the most beautiful parts of the country. The nobility have their summer estates and hunting lodges hereabout. And a few rustic cottages, with all the comforts the rustics themselves never see. It amuses the nobles to play at being peasants. I wonder if they'd be equally amused if the peasants took it into their heads to play at being nobles."

Soon after, Florian pulled up the wagon in the yard of a cluster of buildings screened by woods. The main house was of timber, with a high-pitched roof. Several horses occupied the stables; two more stood tethered near a stone-sided well.

Stock was sitting on a barrel by the door. He jumped off and hurried to the wagon. Justin and Zara climbed down and went directly inside, seeming to be familiar with the place.

"You have visitors," Stock announced to Florian. Theo followed them into a long room with white plaster walls and a huge fireplace. Luther was there, along with half a dozen men Theo had never seen before. Some wore hunter's garb, with game bags over their shoulders; others, the rough jackets of farm laborers. Fowling pieces and muskets were stacked in a corner.

Two men sat at a plank table, the remains of a meal in front of them: the younger, ill-shaven and glum-looking; his companion, white-haired and with one arm in a sling. Both were grimy, their clothes torn and burr-clotted.

The company warmly greeted Florian, who waved a hand and turned his attention to the men at the table. The younger stood up.

"My name is Keller. We have certain acquaintances in common. Thanks to them, we were put on our way here. Though I have to tell you, sir, you are devilish hard to find."

"I'm glad of that," said Florian. "For my own sake, if not yours. I would have preferred meeting Old Kasperl in easier circumstances."

"You know of me, so far from Marianstat?" Keller's glum expression turned into a delighted smile. "I take that as high praise."

"My traveling companion," Keller went on, "looks like one of his own patients. How that came about he shall tell you himself: Dr. Torrens, formerly court physician, presently an exile—as long as he manages to stay alive. As for the unlikely association of a scrivener with a physician, you may wish to know—"

"I should rather know why a courtier is here at all."

"I can answer that very simply," Dr. Torrens said. "I take it for granted that you despise Chief Minister Cabbarus as much as I do. You know, certainly, that Augustine is now hardly able to rule and may never be. What you do not know, since you are not close to the inner workings of the court, is that Cabbarus schemes to make himself Augustine's adoptive heir. For these six years, the chief minister has been king in all but name. Now he seeks the title as well as the power."

Instead of sharing the doctor's outrage, Florian made a small gesture.

"King Augustine or King Cabbarus? To me, Doctor, kings are one and the same."

"You cannot believe that!" cried Torrens. "Do you see no difference between a monarch and a tyrant? The chief minister has been a disaster for the country. As king, he will be still worse. At court, the only one who dares oppose him is Queen Caroline. Her life may be in danger as a result. Cabbarus will let no one

stand in his way. He has banished me, he has tried to
have me murdered. But I will not leave the kingdom.
I seek honest men to join me and support the queen's
cause, to bring force to bear—"

"Let us understand each other," Florian broke in.
"You are correct on two counts. We are honest men
here. Our opinion of Cabbarus matches yours. As for
supporting your cause, I see no reason. We intend,
Doctor, to support our own."

"Whatever that may be," said Torrens, "it is less urgent than putting an end to the influence of Cabbarus. The villain must be brought down, without delay.
whatever the cost. There is no other way to preserve
legitimate monarchy."

"Preserve it?" returned Florian. "Preserve a power
fixed by an accident of birth? Unearned, unmerited,
only abused? You have been sadly misled, Doctor, if
you come to me for that. Legitimate monarchy? The
only legitimate rulers are the people of Westmark."

"That, sir, is a dream. I do not share it with you.
There are abuses; I do not deny it. They must be cor-
rected. But not through destruction. If I have a patient with a broken leg, I mend the leg. I do not bleed
him to death. I do what is possible and practical."

"So do I," said Florian. "You urge me to join you.
Let me ask: How many troops do you command?
How many weapons?"

"None," said Torrens. "And you?" He gestured toward the stack of firearms. "If that is your arsenal, it
does not impress me."

"We hope to improve it within the next twenty-four
hours. Our resources are modest, but only a beginning. Now, Doctor, if you will excuse me, we have
plans to make."

As much as Florian had spoken bitterly and angrily
against the chief minister, Theo had never until now
heard him oppose the whole monarchy. The idea

stunned and excited him. The sheer daring of it was only what he might have expected from Florian. He suddenly understood his willingness to make the journey to Nierkeeping. The man's boldness dazzled him. It also horrified him.

"You're going to attack the town!" cried Theo. "You said you'd help my friends."

"So I will," Florian said. "Did you imagine we'd simply stroll into Nierkeeping and ask politely to have them set loose?"

"No. But not this way. There's going to be bloodshed."

"That's certain. Some of ours. Some of theirs. As little as possible, but no avoiding it. Yes, youngster, it may end with killing. We'd be a band of innocent idiots if we didn't expect it. You want your friends. My people want guns. We'll do whatever we must. Will you?"

Theo did not reply. Florian looked at him and said quietly, "It's very simple. Are you going with us or not? You need our help, but we need yours if my plan has any chance of working."

Theo turned away. He had tried to kill the Royal Inspector in the heat of anger, unthinking. What Florian asked of him was something calculated, accepted in advance. Yet he could not bring himself to abandon Mickle, or even Las Bombas and Musket. He tried to guess what Anton would have done. He could not. He had no answer, nor could any answer have satisfied him; and that, more than anything, tore at him. Finally, without speaking, he nodded his head.

"You'll get through it," said Florian. "The first time is the worst."

Stock, meanwhile, had brought a wooden chest to the table and had begun taking pistols from it. Florian handed one to Theo, who drew back a little.

"It won't bite you," said Florian.

"I don't want it."

"Take it, even so. You may not want it, but you may need it. Do you know how to use one?"

Theo shook his head.

"Go along with Justin, then. He'll show you."

17

It was still dark when they left the farm: Theo and
Justin, Stock and Zara in the wagon; Florian and the
rest of the company on horseback. A short distance
from town, Zara halted in the shadow of a gravel embankment. Florian embraced each one, and they
parted there—Florian to lead his men into Nierkeeping from another quarter, Theo and the others to go
the rest of the way on foot.

Justin strode out eagerly, urging them to speed their
pace until Zara told him to be quiet. Stock yawned
and grumbled at being abroad in the dregs of the
night.

Once within the town limits, no one spoke. Theo
clenched his jaws to keep his teeth from chattering.
The chill of the hours at the thin edge of daybreak
had seeped into his bones. The pistol butt drove into
his belly at every step. Following Luther's directions,
they passed through a winding lane and soon reached
the square. In the middle of it stood a narrow cage
hardly taller than the shape inside.

Theo broke from the others and ran across the
square. The cage reeked like an animal's pen. The

man inside groaned. It was Las Bombas, hardly recognizable. His lips were swollen and split, a stubble of beard covered his cheeks. Theo grappled the bars. The count hunched up his shoulders and turned his face away.

"Let me be."

"It's all right," whispered Theo. "We're going to get you out."

The count shifted his position and raised his head. His voice was raw and rasping. "Who's that? My dear boy, is it you?" He put his hands through the bars and passed his fingers over Theo's face. "Merciful heaven, so it is!"

Stock and Justin had come up behind Theo. Zara followed. She crouched and peered into the cage, then wrinkled her face.

"Is this what we've come to rescue?"

"Shut up, Zara," Theo flung back. "You know Florian's plan. He wants a diversion. He'll have one. But this man's my friend, even so."

The count was pleading for water. Theo pulled the flask from his belt and passed it through the bars. Las Bombas seized it and downed the contents in one gulp. "Thank you, my boy. You've saved my life. It's gone badly with us since you left. But now that you're back again—"

"Not to stay. I'm working in Freyborg. I heard you were in trouble."

"Don't leave us again. We need you. Mickle's lost spirit, she won't do The Oracle Priestess. Nothing's worked right, not even this: The Escaping Prisoner. Nothing simpler. A sheet over the cage, an instant later I'm out, lock untouched, no key in sight. Marvelous effect. It would have gone splendidly if some blockhead hadn't made me open my mouth. They found the picklock I'd hidden there.

"Stupid yokels! Claimed I was cheating them. They said I promised to escape and they'd leave me here until I did. Mickle tried to open the lock, but they caught her at it and threw her in jail, with Musket for good measure."

"We'll see to them now and come back for you," Theo said. "What became of Friska and the coach?"

"In the blacksmith's stable, near the barracks."

Theo glanced at Stock, who nodded agreement and set off immediately across the square.

Zara stood up. "Are the two of you ready?"

Theo hurried after Justin, with Zara at his heels. The jail, as Luther had told them, was at the back of the town hall. They found it easily. At the door of the guardroom, Theo halted and gripped Justin by the scruff of the neck.

"Don't act up yet," he whispered. "Wait until we're inside and see how many we have to deal with. Then start shouting your head off."

Zara stayed back. Theo tightened his grasp on Justin and hauled him through the door. One constable drowsed at a table. At a glance from Theo, Justin began struggling and protesting furiously. The startled officer jumped to his feet and seized the pistol in front of him.

"Thief!" Theo hung on to his pretended captive. "I caught him trying to pick my pocket."

"Who the devil are you?" The constable eyed him suspiciously. He waved his pistol. "You're not from around here, neither of you."

"I'm staying at the inn," Theo said hastily. "I've just come from—from Freyborg. I'd no sooner set foot in town than this fellow tries to rob me. I'll see him behind bars. Lock him up, officer. I'll swear charges against him."

"No business of mine. He's not one of our thieves."

The constable frowned. "As for you, let's see your travel permit."

At this instant, Zara burst into the guardroom, weeping and wringing her hands. "Sir, that's my brother. He meant no harm. I beg you, don't take him away."

The officer hesitated, uncertain whether to deal first with the distraught young woman or the thief and his captor. Adding to the man's confusion, Justin broke loose and Theo made a show of trying to recapture him. The constable spun around, groping for one, then the other.

Zara chose this moment to dart behind the table. She picked up the chair and brought it down on the constable's head. The constable dropped to his knees. Theo leaped on him and locked his hands around the man's throat. "Keys! Where?"

The constable motioned with his head. A ring of keys hung on the wall beside a rack of muskets. Justin had begun ripping away the man's shirt.

"Who's with you?" demanded Theo.

"Alone," gasped the officer. "Night watch. Nobody else."

Theo tore off the man's neck stock and crammed it into the constable's mouth. He beckoned Zara to finish trussing up the officer with the strips of shirt. He snatched the ring and raced down a short flight of steps. Iron-studded doors lined the corridor. Theo fumbled with the keys and found one to unlock the first cell. Musket was inside.

"Go to the marketplace!" cried Theo. "Stay with the count."

The dwarf asked no questions. He took to his heels and dashed up the steps. Theo snapped open the lock on the next cell. Mickle stared at him. Her face was dirty and haggard. Straw from the cell floor clung to her hair.

He held out his arms, but Mickle gave him a haughty glance and drew away.

"Come out! Hurry!" Theo shouted. "What's wrong with you?"

"Don't touch me," Mickle flung back. "You went off without a word! Not a word to me! You can go to the devil, for all I care."

Seizing the girl by the shoulders, Theo pulled her from the cell and sent her stumbling up the stairs ahead of him. Outside, he clamped a hand around her arm and half dragged her, still in icy silence, toward the square.

A shot rang from the direction of the barracks. He glimpsed Justin and Zara beside the cage, along with Musket. More shots rattled through the still air and the clatter of hooves. He glanced back. Friska was galloping into the marketplace, the coach jolting behind her. Stock, upright on the box, was roaring at the top of his voice. By now, Theo judged, the Nierkeeping garrison must be awake and tumbling out of the barracks.

This was the moment Florian and his company had counted on to break into the arsenal holding the garrison's store of weapons. Theo had given Florian his diversion. Now he could turn his efforts to setting Las Bombas free and rely on the others to help him. Whatever else happened, Florian had ordered them to get clear of the town and rejoin him at the farm.

Mickle twisted away and ran to the cage. Swearing furiously, she struggled with the lock. Meantime, Stock had pulled up Friska. He jumped down and went toward Zara. The dressmaker, like Justin, carried two muskets, seized from the rack in the guardroom. She tossed one to the poet.

"To the wagon!" shouted Stock. "If the lock won't open, we'll drag him out, cage and all."

Mickle's face was streaked with grime and sweat. "I can't do it without tools. Hanno knew how, but I don't. Damn him for getting himself hanged!"

Stock rummaged in his pockets and brought out a penknife. He threw it to the girl. Mickle set to work again. The blade snapped in two. She spat and flung it away.

Soldiers from the garrison had begun pouring into the marketplace. Mickle jumped to her feet and ran to Zara. She tore at the dressmaker's shawl.

"This should do it." She seized Zara's brooch and slid the point of the pin into the lock. She turned it deftly, one way then another. The cage opened. Mickle crowed in triumph.

Theo and Musket sprang to haul out the count, who was barely able to crawl from his narrow prison. Las Bombas threw his arms around Mickle. "Bless you for a housebreaker!"

"Go, the rest of you," Theo ordered Zara. "Get out of here. We'll catch up with you."

Las Bombas had slipped to the cobbles. Even with the help of Mickle and the dwarf, Theo could scarcely put the count on his feet and heave him into the coach.

Stock and Zara had already started off, with Justin following. After a few paces, Justin suddenly halted and turned back.

He had unslung one of his muskets. His eyes shone with a terrible joy. Before Theo could stop him, Justin flung himself to the cobbles and began firing at the soldiers.

"You fool!" shouted Theo. "Get in the coach!"

That same instant, Theo caught sight of horses milling through the rear ranks of the troops. He thought, first, that cavalry had joined the fray. Then he saw they were riderless and unsaddled. Florian had not

only stormed the arsenal. His company had broken
into the stables to send the animals galloping in panic
among the soldiers.

The ranks broke and scattered at the threat of being
trampled. One officer, bawling for his men to advance, beat at them with the flat of his saber until he
managed to lead some of them clear of the stampede.

The officer ran toward the coach. Justin fired
again. He missed his mark. The man was on top of
him in a moment. Justin scrambled to his feet. He
tried to fend off the saber stroke with his musket. The
force of the blow knocked the weapon from his hands.
By the time Theo reached him, the officer had
brought up his blade again. Had Theo not pulled Justin aside, the saber would have struck him in the
throat. Instead, it laid open the lad's forehead and
cheek. The man braced to make another attack.

"Kill him!" Justin turned his bloody face to Theo,
violet eyes blazing. "Kill him!"

Theo swung up his arm and leveled the pistol. He
hesitated an instant. Justin was screaming for him to
shoot. Theo cried out as the explosion echoed through
his head. A look of bewilderment froze on the officer's face. He staggered and fell. Theo stared at the
weapon in his hand. His finger had not moved on the
trigger.

He glanced up to see Florian. He was on horseback,
a smoking musket across the saddlebow. His long hair
hung matted, smears of gunpowder blackened his
cheeks. His gray eyes fixed squarely on Theo. He half
smiled, as if observing a child fumbling to tie a shoe.

Florian motioned with his head toward Justin. "See
to him."

He wheeled his horse back across the square. The
rest of his company had galloped into the marketplace
in the wake of the riderless mounts, driving them to-

ward the oustkirts of the town. The soldiers, regroup-
ing, sent volleys of musketry after the raiders, who
sharply returned their fire. Florian's men pressed their
retreat, leaving half a dozen of the garrison sprawled
on the cobblestones.

Theo flung away his pistol. Mickle was beside him.
Between them, they dragged Justin into the coach.
Friska plunged forward.

PART FOUR
The Garden of Cabbarus

18

Out of respect for his position, the chief minister allowed himself certain small luxuries. One of these was a private garden that yielded, in all seasons, blossoms of information. Cabbarus fertilized it with generous applications of money. The harvest was always more plentiful and usually more accurate than the labored, vegetablelike reports of provincial constables and police spies. Cabbarus earnestly believed his rank entitled him to this higher quality of produce. Since he cultivated his garden personally, he saw no reason to share it.

As in the most carefully tended gardens, the occasional weed sprang up or plant withered. Cabbarus had his disappointments. The individual he counted on to deal with Torrens had not thrived. This in itself did not trouble the chief minister. As a precaution, the man would have been pruned, in any case. What nettled Cabbarus was that he had no inkling of the doctor's fate.

Torrens and his opponent might have killed each other. Cabbarus found that unlikely. The court physician might have fallen from the embankment and

been borne away on the tide. But no corpse had sur-
faced. The chief minister's informants could report
only that Torrens had vanished. Cabbarus was not
pleased to accept this. No one truly vanished except
by the chief minister's order.

Nevertheless, until he heard otherwise, Cabbarus
counted Torrens as dead—if not in fact, for all practical purposes. The king required his urgent attention.
Augustine was presenting difficulties.

First, the king had no recollection of banishing Torrens and called for the court physician to attend him.

"He grievously offended Your Majesty," said Cabbarus. "Your Majesty had no choice but to dismiss him."

"No matter. I desire him back again."

Cabbarus assured his monarch it was impossible. For
some days, however, Augustine continued to demand
the presence of the physician. Finally, he let the matter drop. But he refused the services of any other doctor, even those whom Cabbarus highly recommended.
The king's health improved alarmingly.

His mind, too, grew somewhat clearer. Cabbarus
blamed this on the occultists, necromancers, and spiritualists; rather, on the lack of them. What had been a
constant procession dwindled to a handful.

"The reward is still not adequate," Augustine declared. "I direct you to double the sum."

"As Your Majesty commands." Cabbarus bowed his
head. Since he was sure the reward would go un-
claimed, he had no objection to doubling, or even tre-
bling it. "It shall be so proclaimed."

"You shall add one thing further to the proclamation. As we offer a reward for success, we judge it
fitting, as well, to impose a penalty for failure."

"I do not entirely understand, Sire. A penalty? Of
what nature?"

"These men have claimed spiritual powers, but they

have disappointed me beyond bearing. Nevertheless, they have been enriched by their failures. Now it is my command: If they accomplish nothing, they are to be paid nothing."

"As Your Majesty so aptly expresses it, this is only fitting. They shall not be paid."

"That is not the penalty."

"What then, Sire?"

"If they fail," said the king, "they shall be put to death."

"Majesty," exclaimed Cabbarus, "a penalty of such severity—"

"A severe punishment for severe disappointment," said Augustine. "Proclaim it, Chief Minister. I command you to do so."

The king held to that point in spite of the chief minister's protests. Cabbarus, for all his influence, could not move him to revoke it. Cabbarus devoutly believed in punishment, but in this case he saw the consequences immediately. There were rogues aplenty who would venture anything for gain. There was an even greater number of fools. Finding a combination of the two was another matter. No rogue would be foolish enough to risk his neck attempting the impossible. The penalty for failure ended all visitations.

Worse, the court physician had been right. Without the daily arrival of charlatans to feed his obsession, Augustine recovered some of his former calm.

Cabbarus fumed inwardly. The proclamation showed that Augustine was regaining some of his wits. For the good of the kingdom, Cabbarus wished its ruler would suffer a relapse. But wishes, Cabbarus knew, seldom came true without enterprise on the part of the wisher. Throughout his private garden, he planted word that he required a fresh supply of necromancers. The seeds did not sprout.

For several weeks, the chief minister showed every sign of cheerfulness. In the same way that he cloaked his pleasure in frowns, he wreathed his fury in smiles. His good humor astonished the courtiers. As usual, only Pankratz appreciated how matters really stood. A smiling Cabbarus was a dangerous Cabbarus.

Pankratz, therefore, dealt very gingerly with his master. Cabbarus, in private, made little attempt to hide his feelings. Not long before, over some inconsequential failing, Cabbarus had struck his councillor full in the face. Pankratz merely rubbed his jowls and bowed his way out of the minister's chambers. The Minister's Mastiff accepted that dogs were made to be occasionally beaten. He respected his master all the more for it, and passed along the chief minister's bad temper, in kind, to his own underlings.

Nevertheless, Pankratz held himself at arm's length one evening when he announced that a certain individual desired a private audience.

Cabbarus, in his apartments, had just finished supper and it was not sitting happily with him. In any case, he disliked conducting business directly with his creatures. It made him feel that he had put his fingers into something disagreeable: a task better entrusted to Councillor Pankratz. Cabbarus shook his head.

"I do not wish to see him. Let him discuss the matter with you."

"Excellency, he insists." Pankratz half bowed and spread his hands in a gesture both deferential and defensive. "It has to do with—what Your Excellency has been inquiring about."

The chief minister's eyes flickered an instant with excitement. He kept his face impassive. "I doubt that he offers much of value. However, as he insists, you may send him to me." He motioned with his head. "Below."

Cabbarus put on his robe and made his way without haste to one of the cellars of the Old Juliana. It had once been a torture chamber. None of the instruments remained. They had been dismantled during the reign of Augustine the Great—a wastefulness Cabbarus would never have allowed had he been in office at the time. Iron rings and staples, however, had been left in the walls. In one corner, a wooden trapdoor offered an opening somewhat larger than the girth of a man. It was the mouth of a deep well, roughly faced with stones and mortar.

Although the bottom of this well was too heavily shadowed to be seen, a torrent of water could be heard. The shaft tapped into an underground stream whose course had never been fully traced. Presumably it flowed to join the Vespera. It once had served as a means of disposing of prisoners or portions of them. The flagstones around the trap sloped inward, making it easier to wash down the chamber floor and send the sweepings into the shaft.

The present Augustine had commanded the well to be bricked over and sealed at the same time he had ordered the Juliana Bells to be silenced. The latter order had been carried out, but not the former. Cabbarus had taken it on himself to ignore it. The chief minister found it pointless to destroy such a useful feature merely because of the king's hindsight.

Awaiting his guest, the chief minister stood by the trapdoor, studying it thoughtfully. When Cabbarus granted a rare personal audience, he always chose this chamber. There was no mistaking what it had been, and it impressed his visitors with the seriousness of their endeavors.

He glanced up as Councillor Pankratz ushered in the man, then went to sit behind a heavy oaken table. Pankratz discreetly vanished. Cabbarus did not invite his guest to be seated, and eyed him silently for several moments.

The man was short and stout. Perspiration filmed his plump cheeks. Cabbarus noted the fur-trimmed cloak and the gold chain around his visitor's neck.

"You have, I see, bettered your station in life," said Cabbarus. "I believe you formerly went about as a tinker."

"That is correct, sir," the man replied. "It served its purpose. Alderman, though, carries more weight and substance. It conveys, you might say, the aroma of prosperity. It suits well enough at the moment."

"Your choice of profession is up to you. Get on with your business. You say you have found a ghost-raiser."

"Ah, well, sir, perhaps I have and perhaps I haven't."

"I urge you," said Cabbarus, "to decide which, and to do so quickly."

"Well, sir, you see it's a curious thing. A few months ago I was in Kessel, and I came upon a knave calling himself, if memory serves, Bloomsa. He took me for a greater fool than himself. He had the impudence to swindle me. Try to, that is."

"And you, naturally, ended up swindling him."

"As you say, sir, naturally." The man allowed himself a wink. "But that only begins the tale. I thought no more of him until a while after. I happened to be passing through a town called Felden. The local gossip was all about a fellow who had made quite a splash there. Some sort of flummery: spirit apparitions, a wench playing at being an oracle, and all such great nonsense.

"He was doing well for himself until something happened, I don't know what. The wench, for some reason, turned skittish. In any case, the novelty wore off. But the fellow had run up a fortune in bills. His creditors started coming down on him. They'd have thrown him in jail. He saved them the trouble by leaving one night—in something of a hurry. From what the Feld-

eners told me of him, I thought: Aha, here's Master
Bloomsa up to another of his tricks.

"The constables were still searching his lodgings.
He and his crew had gone off so quickly the constables thought they might find some valuables left
behind. Out of curiosity, I did a little poking about,
too.

"It's a matter of nose, sir," continued the self-styled
alderman, tapping his own. "My nose told me there
might be something of interest, though I didn't know
what. I trust my nose, sir, and always follow it. This
time, I fear it disappointed me. There was nothing
worth mention. Except one thing. I took it along.
Again I don't know why. The nose advised me, very
likely."

The chief minister's patience had worn threadbare.
He was about to tell the man to take his nose and
himself to the devil. Then his visitor drew a rumpled
sheet of paper from his cloak and spread it on the table.

"The Feldeners tell me it's a good enough likeness."

It was a portrait of a young girl. Only by effort was
the chief minister able to compose himself.

"And so, sir," the man was going on, "when I later
heard you were looking for ghost-raisers, I wondered
if our Master Bloomsa might be of some use after all,
especially with the wench."

Cabbarus barely heard him. He was engrossed in
the portrait. Once more, his confidence had been jus-
tified. Opportunity always arose when it was needed.
He suddenly understood how simple it was. He need
no longer be concerned with forcing the queen's approval, or even being named adoptive heir. The answer lay within reach. Cabbarus nearly did something
he had seldom done in all his life. He nearly laughed.
Instead, he scowled with joy.

"Where are they now?"

The visitor shrugged. "There's the difficulty, sir. I didn't follow them, you see. Had I known you'd be wanting someone in that line of work, I'd have kept a finger on them. Now it may take some doing, as the trail is cold. And so I came to ask your instructions, sir. If you think it worth the time and toil—and the money."

"Find them," said Cabbarus. "I want them."

19

Musket, clearly experienced in avoiding pursuit, did not trouble to ask their destination. He drove Friska at top speed and sent the coach careening through the outskirts of the town, deep into the countryside, up and down lanes hardly suitable for an oxcart. Justin, sprawled across the seat, was bleeding heavily. Mickle had torn a strip from her dress and, despite the jolting vehicle, tried to stanch the wound.

Theo helped her, his hands moving mechanically. The girl barely spoke to him. His joy at finding her was gone. Half his thoughts were in Nierkeeping. He still saw the bodies in the square, and himself ready to fire the pistol. Justin, too, could have been killed. His bloody face was a silent reproach. Theo raged at himself. He should have pulled the trigger. He wanted to beg forgiveness. Unconscious, Justin could not have heard him.

Musket, judging they had outdistanced any troopers who might have followed, reined up Friska and ran to ask Theo where he wanted to go. The dwarf had saved them and, at the same time, lost them. Theo climbed out and tried to regain his bearings in the unfamiliar countryside.

Las Bombas took the opportunity to stretch his cramped legs. His uniform was wrinkled and befouled, his cheeks sunken. He had perked up enough, however, to brush the grit from his moustache.

"You were right, my boy. Honesty is the best policy. That cage was a blessing in disguise. Public humiliation, private starvation! I vowed to mend my ways if ever I got free. My ordeal reduced me in body, but fortified me in spirit."

Since Theo carried no food and there was none in the coach, Las Bombas had further occasion to fortify his spirit. He climbed back into the coach, resigned to the benefits of continued hunger. Justin had turned restless. Las Bombas held him in his arms and soothed him with a gentleness Theo had never suspected.

Their only choice, Theo decided, was to circle back and, in spite of risk, find the Nierkeeping road. He jumped onto the box beside Musket and tried to guide him. Partly by luck, partly by the dwarf's own sense of direction, they finally came upon it. Theo recognized the fingerpost where Florian had turned. They followed the road into the hills. Even then, they would have missed the farm if some of Florian's men, stationed as guards, had not shown them the rest of the way.

It was late afternoon when they rolled into the farmyard. Florian was in the doorway. Though obviously relieved to see them, he exchanged only the briefest greetings. He himself carried Justin into the house. Stock, Zara, and the others were sorting the captured weapons.

The court physician had been standing by the fireplace. He went immediately to examine Justin's wound and called for clean bandages and a basin of water.

"More bloodshed." Torrens glanced up at Florian. "I have seen enough of it this day."

"So have I," said Florian. "You forget, I was at Nier-keeping, too. And let me remind you: You were not much impressed, yesterday, by our modest store of arms. Perhaps now you have changed your opinion. In any case, I lost three of my best men. Do your work, Doctor. I don't want to lose a fourth."

Florian turned away. Seeing Mickle, he smiled and bowed gracefully. "So this must be the young lady in question?"

"I didn't know there was any question about me," said Mickle.

"This is Florian," said Theo. "Without him, you'd still be in jail."

"And with him," replied Mickle, "we nearly got shot. He's dangerous."

Florian laughed. "I sincerely hope I am. But only to my enemies. You're quite safe. I suggest you go along with Zara and see if she can find something better for you to wear."

"We are in your debt, sir," put in Las Bombas. "I must say your line of work entails certain, ah, hazards. I should be glad to provide you with special remedies of my own preparation, at wholesale rates."

When Florian declined the offer, Las Bombas turned his attention to the larder.

Theo took Florian's arm. "There's something I have to know—about what happened this morning."

"We couldn't have done without you," said Florian. "We needed that fracas of yours to draw off the garri-son. You have your friends back; we have guns and horses. We paid a price. Does that still trouble you? Believe me, it could have been worse."

"It's not only that. It's Justin. You saved his life."

"Luckily. What of it?"

"I should have. I was there beside him. I should have been the one to do it."

Florian shook his head. "Justin won't worry over who takes the credit."

"If anything," replied Theo, "he'll be proud it was you. But the man was right in front of me. I had the pistol."

"And you held back," said Florian. "I saw you. Beware, youngster. Next time, don't hesitate. It may cost your life."

"But you," said Theo. "You didn't hesitate. You shot him without having to think."

"Some things are best not thought about."

"I have to," said Theo. "I have to understand. You know what happened in Dorning. I swore then I'd never try to take another man's life. Killing is wrong. I believed that. I still do. But now I wonder. Do I believe it because I want to be a decent man? Or— because I'm a coward?"

"In which case, you're no different from the rest of us." Florian gave a wry smile. "We're all afraid. And afraid of being afraid. You'll get used to it."

"I don't want to get used to it," cried Theo. "If I'd really known what it would be like—"

"You wouldn't have gone to Nierkeeping? Would you rather see your friends still in jail? Starving in a cage? And even if you'd shot that officer, what then? Half his trade is killing; the other half, being killed."

"The first day I met you," said Theo, "at Rina's birthday party, you said there was only one law, that all men are brothers."

Florian nodded. "Yes. And sometimes brothers kill each other. For the sake of justice. For the sake of a higher cause."

"Who decides what's right? Me? You? Dr. Torrens? He's against you. He holds with the monarchy. But he seems a good and honorable man."

"He is," answered Florian. "Curious that being a commoner he should take that side. Perhaps he knows less of it than I do. I can tell you of peasants flogged half to death, forced to weed a noble's garden while their own crops rot in the ground, having their cottages pulled down to make room for a deer park. I know the aristocracy better than Torrens ever can. I was born into it.

"Yes," Florian went on, smiling at Theo's astonishment. "You might recognize my family's name if I mentioned it, which, by the way, I have no intention of doing. This farm is theirs. They've forgotten they even own it, among so many others. They would be highly displeased if they knew the purpose it served.

"As for Torrens thinking merely to correct abuses— he is almost as innocent as you are. Abuse is in the very grain of the monarchy's power. And I can tell you one thing more. Men give up many things willingly: their fortunes, their loves, their dreams. Power, never. It must be taken. And you, youngster, will have to choose your side. Though I assure you the monarchy will be as unsparing with its enemies as I am, at least there is justice in my cause."

"Even if the cuase if good," said Theo, "what does it do to the people who stand against it? And the people who follow it?"

"Next time you see Jellinek," said Florian, "ask him if he's ever found a way to make an omelet without breaking eggs."

"Yes," Theo said. "Yes, but men aren't eggs."

20

Dr. Torrens was calling Florian, who left Theo unanswered and went anxiously to the court physician.

"The lad is in no danger now," said Torrens, rolling down his sleeves. He had taken off the sling and crammed it into his pocket. "Though I fear he will be badly scarred."

"We may all be," said Florian. He strode to the table and called the rest to join him.

"My children," he said to Stock and Zara, "we'd best take leave of each other for a while. Our worthy opponents in Nierkeeping had too close a look at me. After today's business, I can't even risk staying in Freyborg. You two should be safe enough there. For me, the wiser course is to disappear. Better to be wanted than found. Give my greetings to Jellinek. Tell him I shall miss those concoctions he fancifully calls stew. You shall have word from me later. Take some of the muskets. We shall find a good hiding place for the remainder. Justin will stay with me. Luther, too."

He turned to the court physician. "And you, Doctor? We have our differences. I suggest, for the time being, we bury them—if you will forgive my using the term with a physician. We are both marked men. If caught, we shall be equally dead. We can agree on that much."

Torrens nodded. "Who knows, you may change your views, or I, mine. I judge either unlikely. Indeed, sir, the day may come when we find each other very bad companions. Until then, I shall go with you."

"Since I've brought Dr. Torrens this far," put in Keller, "I think the time has come for the Bear to go into hibernation; and for Old Kasperl to make his way with the doctor and yourself."

"Old Kasperl would keep us amused," said Florian. "But if he is silenced, then Cabbarus might as well have hanged you. You would do greater service if you kept on with your journal."

"Gladly," said Keller. "But without the means, it is impossible. For one thing, I would have to stay hidden."

"Old Kasperl and the Bear can find a safe lair in Freyborg," said Florian. "Trust my children for that."

"Even so, a journalist is nothing without a press. Nothing, sometimes, with one. But it is essential to the trade."

"You shall have a press in Freyborg," replied Florian. "Whether you may also have a printer"—he glanced at Theo—"I leave it up to this young man. He may want to talk over the matter with his friends. Do it quickly, youngster. We must all be gone before daybreak."

"Meantime," said Las Bombas, wiping his plate clean with a slice of bread, "I should welcome an opportunity for professional discourse with a colleague."

"Do you refer to me, sir?" Torrens raised an eyebrow. "I was not aware that we were colleagues in any way at all."

"We are both men of science," the count replied. "That is, in our respective endeavors. My present endeavor is for my coachman and me to leave the country at the earliest possible moment. I feel things are pressing in upon us a little too closely for comfort. Trebizonia, a realm long familiar to me during my attendance on the prince, will surely welcome my services."

Mickle and Zara had come into the room. Zara had given the girl an old woolen skirt, a man's jacket, and a shawl. Zara went to Florian's side. Mickle strode out of the farmhouse. Leaving Las Bombas to expound his scientific discoveries to the court physician, Theo followed her.

Dusk was gathering quickly. The trees had not yet dropped all their leaves and the ragged branches laid heavy shadows across the yard. He heard Musket working in the stables and Friska whinnying among the tethered horses.

Mickle stood near the well. She had pulled the shawl closer around her shoulders. He called to her. The girl turned and looked coolly at him. She had grown even thinner. The oversized garments seemed to hold a bundle of sticks.

"Florian wants me to go back to Freyborg," Theo began. "That's where I've been living, since—"

"Since you ran off without so much as a fare-thee-well," said Mickle. "You had me thinking you liked me. Next thing I knew, you were gone."

"I didn't want to leave."

"Then why did you?"

"I thought it was best. There's a lot you don't know about me."

"I doubt it," Mickle said. "The count told me why you took up with him. Zara told me the rest."

"Well, then you see why I couldn't ask you to come with me. I'm a criminal; the police are looking for me. I could be arrested any time. By now, I suppose, I would have been. If Florian hadn't helped me."

"The police are looking for everybody I know," Mickle said. "That's not much of a reason."

"For me it is. Suppose they'd caught me? They'd have arrested you, too."

"It's happened before. I'm used to it."

"I'm not. I'm not used to anything that's happened to me. I'm not used to hoaxing gullible people, or pretending to be a High Brazilian savage—"

"You were very good at it." Mickle grinned for the first time since their meeting.

"That's the trouble, don't you see? When I ran into the count, I thought it would be a chance to see the rest of the world. That's really what I wanted. Not swindling people with elixirs made from ditch water, or claiming to raise ghosts. Least of all, trying to kill someone. But I've done all that. Even getting you out of jail, I lied like a thief. Worse, it didn't bother me at all. What kind of person does that make me?"

"No different from anyone else," Mickle said. "Did you think you were?"

"I don't know. I don't know what I am anymore."

"Tell me when you find out," said Mickle. "As you're so itchy to go traveling, I suppose you'll run off again."

"That can wait. I have work to do in Freyborg now."

"That's fine for you," said Mickle. "You needn't wonder what becomes of me."

"I thought—I took it for granted you'd stay with the count and Musket."

"You could ask, at least."

"Will you come to Freyborg with me?"

Theo heard his own voice, not from his lips but seeming to come from the bottom of the well. Taken aback for an instant, he realized it was Mickle. The girl was laughing.

"I'm not the phrenological head," protested Theo,

laughing himself. "You needn't put words in my mouth."

"You weren't putting them there yourself."

"All right," said Theo. "Will you come with me? What else happens, I don't care. Florian wants to bring down the monarchy, Torrens wants to patch it up, the count's off to humbug the Trebizonians. All I want is—I don't want us to be apart anymore."

He thought she was still laughing at him when he put his arms around her. He was surprised to discover, then, what he had not been able to see in the dark. The girl's cheeks were wet.

"It's bad enough crying when I'm asleep," said Mickle. "Why should I do it when I'm awake?"

21

At first light, Florian and his party said their farewells. Justin, bandaged and pale but looking very proud, had been given one of the cavalry mounts. Florian sat astride a bay mare with a blanket for a saddle.

"Do well, youngster," he said to Theo. "I count on you for that."

Theo watched them ride from the farmyard. Florian had still not given him the honor of calling him his child. Theo was uncertain whether to be sorry or glad.

Zara, Stock, and Keller left soon after. Theo and Mickle would have gone in the cart with them, but Las Bombas, for the sake of old times, insisted on driving them to Freyborg in the coach. While Musket hitched up Friska, Theo stayed at Mickle's side. The two had not ceased talking since breakfast, using Mickle's private sign language, so none of the company realized they were in fact chattering like a pair of magpies.

Theo had put aside his own anxieties. He was happy, with no room in his mind for them. He was impatient for Mickle to see the Strawmarket cubbyhole, Jellinek's tavern, the press, as if these were treasures he had been storing up for her.

Las Bombas had changed his ruined uniform for the robes of Dr. Absalom. He had slept well, eaten still better, and had trimmed his moustache into something close to jauntiness.

"I urge you both to reconsider," he told Theo and Mickle as they climbed into the coach. "A fascinating country, Trebizonia. I promise you, my boy, no oracles, no undines, not even Dr. Absalom's Elixir. I intend to follow the path of virtue. It will not be overcrowded."

Seeing his persuasive powers had no effect, Las Bombas sighed and settled into a corner of the coach. The day promised to be sharp and bright. Musket set off at a walking pace, looking for a road that would carry them north and, as well, give Nierkeeping the widest berth.

The Demon Coachman's instincts for the lay of the land proved sound. Before noon, he struck a good highway several leagues above Nierkeeping. By luck, there was a posthouse at the crossroads. Friska needed fodder and water. Las Bombas required something more substantial. Musket reined up, but the count now realized he was suffering from the return of an old ailment.

"I haven't a penny to my name. Honesty tends to reduce one's cash in hand. But wait—this may answer: my lodestone from Kazanastan, from the Mountain of the Moon. It's worth a king's ransom. If I can remember where I put it, I'd be willing to part with it for a modest sum."

He rummaged in a box under the seat and at last brought out the black, egg-sized pebble which Theo recognized from their first meeting. The count's good resolutions were still too new and unexercised to withstand his appetite. He would hear none of Theo's objections, and strode into the public room. Mickle and Theo followed reluctantly, with Musket behind them.

The uncrowded room gave the count a meager choice of customers. At a table, some travelers were playing a game of dominoes. One of them, with several stacks of coins in front of him, was clearly winning handsomely over his opponents. Las Bombas, about to approach, suddenly halted. He stared at the winning player, a pudgy man with a gold chain around his neck.

"See that rascal?" Las Bombas gripped Theo's arm. "That villain sitting there as bold as brass?"

It took Theo a moment to recall the inn at Kessel and the false alderman. Las Bombas muttered, "He robbed me then. He'll pay for it now, with interest. There's justice in the world, after all. Forgiveness is a virtue, but I'll forgive him some other time. Wretch! He's likely rigged those dominoes in some fashion, to fleece innocent wayfarers. They'll be grateful to me for warning them."

"Let him be," whispered Theo. "We don't dare stir up trouble. Get out. We'll find another inn."

Las Bombas had already started for the table. Robes flapping, he shook his fist in the air.

"Gentlemen, I denounce this creature for what he is: a cheat and a fraud! He swindled me out of a fortune and is doing the same to you. Alderman, is he? Thimblerigger! Stand up, Skeit, and deny it if you dare!"

The count's outburst brought players and onlookers to their feet. The losers shouted agreement with Las Bombas. The others, seeing a prosperous gentleman defamed by a gross figure in a shabby robe, defended the alderman. The landlord hurried to the table, waving his arms and ordering all of them to settle their differences outside.

Skeit, during this, kept his seat and his composure.
He was staring at Las Bombas with a look of joy. Far
from cringing at the count's accusation, he beamed.

"My dear sir! My dear—Bloomsa, I believe? This is
the happiest of meetings. Indeed, sir, I had been hoping our paths might cross. I have, in fact, been at
some pains to make sure they did. I would have found
you sooner or later. Now you save me further effort.
This is a moment you will come to regard with a pleasure as great as my own. You, my good Mynheer,
stand to gain a fortune."

At this word, Las Bombas pricked up his ears. He
hesitated, then glared at the self-styled alderman.

"You cannot turn me from my duty. Fortune, you
say? No, you'll not wiggle away by trying to corrupt
me. On the other hand, as a just and reasonable man,
I must in all fairness let you state your case. I shall
allow you to do so in private."

The commotion had brought the rest of the company to the group of quarreling travelers. An army
captain shouldered his way to Las Bombas and
peered at him.

"Sir, do we not know each other?"

"Eh?" Las Bombas gave him a hasty glance. "Not in
any degree. Be so good as to leave us. This gentleman
and I have a matter to discuss."

"But I recognize you, sir," the officer insisted. "You
are General Sambalo. This is your servant—but I rec-
ollect he was Trebizonian. And yourself, no longer in
uniform—"

"At my tailors'," replied the count in a stifled voice.
Assuming a military bearing, he eyed the captain. "I
was merely testing your memory. An officer must always keep his wits about him. I commend you, sir.
Your commander shall have a glowing report from
me."

"Begging the General's pardon," replied the officer,

"this is most irregular. I heard you accuse this individual. I presume, sir, you will press charges against him. I shall see to it on your behalf."

"Not necessary. I shall deal with him myself."

"Begging the General's pardon again, there is another question. A mere formality. Since you are in plain clothes, I am required to ask for your papers."

"Excellent," said the count. "Very dutiful. They are in my uniform."

"Sir, my orders oblige me. There has been a serious incident at Nierkeeping. Without proper identification, even if it were the field marshal himself, I would be required to place him under arrest. I cannot go against regulations. You, sir, must appreciate that more than anyone."

"I'll see you court-martialed!" cried Las Bombas. "Arrest, indeed! I'll have you drummed out of your regiment."

"The captain is in error," said Skeit. "He will not arrest anyone."

"This is not your business," returned the officer. "Hold your tongue or you'll be under lock and key."

The officer, in the unhappy position of being at odds with a superior, was delighted at the chance to berate a civilian.

Skeit, however, drew a paper from his jacket. "Read this. Do you recognize the signature and seal?"

The officer stared at the document and brought up his hand in a full salute.

Skeit nodded. "You understand I have full authority. This man and his party are indeed under arrest. Not by your command. By mine. They shall be in my custody."

"As you order, sir. The girl, too?"

"All of them," replied Skeit. "And, most assuredly, the girl."

22

"Captain," said Skeit, "report to your commander immediately. Tell him that I require an armed escort for myself and these four."

The domino-players, unwilling to be caught up in a serious matter over their heads, drew away. The false alderman took a pistol from under his cloak.

"This is outrageous!" cried Las Bombas. "The man's a fraud. Authority? That scrap of paper's a forgery. I warn you, captain, I have connections at the highest levels."

The count's protest went unheeded by the officer, who turned on his heel and strode from the inn to carry out Skeit's orders. Had he alone been arrested, Theo would have been less surprised. He had lived in fear of it for months. Skeit had barely glanced at him. The man's eyes, instead, were on Mickle.

The girl appeared unconcerned. She drew her shawl closer around her. Then she made a startled movement and stared, half smiling, past Skeit's head.

"Don't move," a voice commanded. "Stand as you are or you're a dead man. Throw down the pistol."

For that instant. Theo was sure Mickle's ruse had saved them. Skeit stiffened. his face was furious. but he let the gun drop from his hand. Musket scurried to pick up the weapon. Skeit had turned to confront his captor. Seeing no one behind him. without pausing to wonder how he had been tricked, the rudgy man moved with astonishing speed. A booted foot shot out to stamp on the dwarf's reaching hand. Musket roared in pain. Skeit drove a heel into the dwarf's ribs. then snatched up the weapon. Losing all caution. Theo flung himself on the man and shouted for Mickle to run.

The landlord. during this. had seized a blunderbuss from the chimney corner. He aimed the heavy firearm at the girl.

"Stand away," Skeit cried to him. "This is my business."

Theo had fallen back. Skeit held the muzzle of the gun to Theo's head.

"Listen to me, all of you," he muttered through clenched teeth. "I don't want you damaged. but I'll have you one way or another. As for this one," he added, indicating Theo. "he had a hand in getting you out of Nierkeeping. I know that and it's not your concern how I know it. He's mixed up with that band of rebels, and I can turn him over to the military here and now. They'll put him against a wall and shoot him. Or you can all come nicely and quietly, and that other matter stays a friendly little secret among us. That's a fair bargain, wouldn't you say?"

Las Bombas nodded glumly. Skeit lowered his pistol and beamed as if he had concluded a difficult but profitable transaction. "We understand each other, then. It will be all in your best interest. And in mine."

"What do you want from us?" Theo demanded.

"I? Nothing whatever. But other people have something in mind." Skeit winked. "What that may be, you'll have to ask them."

"I should have listened to you, my boy." Las Bombas drew a heavy sigh. "I should have let the little snake cheat them all blind. I rue the day I turned honest."

After assuring the landlord and the frightened onlookers that he would personally undertake to burn their brains if they gossiped about the incident, Skeit calmly ordered the trembling host to put up some hampers of provisions.

That they were captives was, to Theo, all too clear. Not clear at all was the nature of their captivity. When the officer returned with a cavalry escort, Skeit went to great pains over the comfort of his prisoners. He demanded quilts and blankets for them in case the weather turned colder. He did not shackle them, as Theo had expected, but advised them pleasantly that they should consider themselves his guests.

They were allowed, in fact obliged, to ride in the coach. Musket, forbidden to drive, at first stayed with them while Skeit took the reins. Friska turned so skittish under an unfamiliar hand that the dwarf had to climb back onto the box. Theo hoped the Demon Coachman would seize a chance to break free of the escort, but the vehicle was too closely hemmed in by the cavalrymen trotting alongside.

Skeit occasionally sat next to the dwarf, directing him when and where to halt: sometimes at the inn of a small town, or at a posthouse along the road. More often, he stayed inside the coach, where his presence made impossible any serious talk among his prisoners.

Theo and Mickle avoided being overheard by using

the girl's sign language. While their captor drowsed or looked through the window, Mickle's hands made slight, unnoticeable motions.

Her quick fingers told Theo, "I can try to take his pistol."

"Too dangerous," he signaled back.

"What then?"

"I don't know. Wait. Be careful. Our chance may come." Theo's look of despair needed no signal.

Skeit, for his part, was in high good humor. Sure of his prisoners, he brightened with every passing mile. He grew expansive and talkative, as if he were sharing a pleasant journey in the friendliest company.

"Be still, you little snake," muttered Las Bombas. "I can't bear the sight of you, let alone your gabble."

Skeit gave him a wounded glance. "My dear sir, you'll be grateful to me. You don't know it yet, but I'm putting you in the way of making a fortune."

Las Bombas snorted in disbelief. The pudgy man winked at him. "Indeed so. Take my word for it. You'll come out of this a very rich man."

Skeit cheerfully added, "Or a very dead one."

If it suited him, Skeit did not hesitate to commandeer and pay for the use of an entire inn. On the strength of the document he carried, he ordered the guests to find lodgings elsewhere. He then chose the largest room and herded his charges into it. Relays of troopers mounted constant guard at the door and within the room itself.

As much as Theo racked his brain and Mickle recalled every trick she knew of housebreaking, they struck on no plan. Escape, Theo had to admit, was impossible. One thing tormented him more than that. Mickle's nightmares had come back.

The guards, forbidden to speak with their prisoners,

kept stolid, silent watch as the girl tossed violently in
her sleep, wept, and cried out. When Theo made a
move to go to her side, a trooper leveled a musket at
him.

The stages of their journey grew more exhausting.
Skeit seemed to become impatient. One morning, he
roused them well before dawn and ordered the escort
to press on with all speed. In the coach, he kept the
curtains tightly drawn. Theo had ceased to care
whether it was day or night. Only when the coach
halted and Skeit, snapping his fingers, urged his prisoners to climb out, did Theo realize it was sundown.
They were in a courtyard between two high buildings. Mickle, half-asleep, shivered beside him. Las
Bombas blinked.

"Not possible," he whispered. "The little worm's
brought us to Marianstat, to the Juliana. There's the
bell tower. I've seen it enough—from the outside, that
is. No mistake, that's where we are. But—inside?"

Skeit, that moment, was approached by a stocky,
bandy-legged man in court dress.

"Delivered, sir," declared Skeit, "as requested."

"Those?" said the courtier, with a look of distaste.
He handed over a purse, which Skeit immediately
tucked away under his cloak. "Now get out. Don't
show your face around here. Your work is done. Even
so, you should have had them cleaned before the chief
minister sees them."

Theo felt Mickle's hand tighten in his own. Before
he could digest what he heard, a detachment of palace guards fell in around them. They were marched
into the older, fortresslike building, and through a
corridor. The bandy-legged courtier, who had gone
ahead, beckoned them to enter a sparsely furnished
chamber. Behind a table sat a black-robed man study-

ing a sheaf of papers. He continued his work for several moments, then glanced up.

"I am given to understand you have come from our northern provinces. I trust the journey was not fatiguing."

Cabbarus smiled.

23

Theo expected a monster. He saw only a gaunt, thin-lipped man he could have taken for a town clerk or notary. Yet, suddenly, he had a taste of tarnished metal in his mouth. The man reeked of power, it hung in the air around him. Theo felt light-headed. He was choking with what he thought was hatred, then realized how much of it was terror. Still smiling, Cabbarus glanced at each of the captives. His eyes came at last to fix on the girl. He made a small motion with his head. Mickle's cheeks had gone gray. A thready sound rose in her throat. The girl had begun shuddering violently. Afraid she might fall, Theo held her arm.

"Does the young woman require assistance?" asked Cabbarus. "I should have provided refreshment. Forgive my oversight, but I have been at my desk all this day. Councillor Pankratz will see to any of your needs."

Las Bombas was the first to find his voice. "There has been, sir, a deplorable misunderstanding, some judicial error. Our lives have been threatened, we have been brought here as prisoners, for no discernible reason."

"The reason," said Cabbarus, "is very simple. I ordered it. The individual I employed may have been overzealous in his duties, but you are not prisoners."

Las Bombas heaved a sigh of relief. Cabbarus raised his hand and went on.

"Not necessarily prisoners. That remains to be seen. For some days, I have been studying a number of reports. I find that serious charges have been laid against this young man. Assault, attempted murder, armed rebellion—an extensive list."

Cabbarus leafed through his papers. "As for you— not long ago a band of rebels attacked the Nierkeeping garrison. I am led to conclude you were present."

"In a cage!" protested Las Bombas. "And my colleagues were—"

"Freed by the selfsame rebels. By the strict letter of the law, you were, therefore, at the scene of a brutal crime, where nearly a dozen soldiers were killed. You did nothing to prevent it. You offered no assistance to the authorities, you came forward with no information. A tribunal must look severely on your conduct. It would, in fact, have no choice but to sentence you to the extreme penalty.

"I am prepared to order all charges dropped. You and your associates will be released and generously compensated. Depending on how well you are able to serve me. A service which is also a duty."

"I have no duty toward you," broke in Theo. "I've done what I'm charged with. Yes, even attempted murder. But you've done more than attempt it."

"Be quiet, for heaven's sake," whispered the count. "If we have any chance at all, don't ruin it."

Cabbarus was unruffled by Theo's outburst. He appeared, instead, grieved by it. "I am quite aware of those among the king's subjects who accuse me of severity. They do not understand that justice must be

severe for the sake of a higher cause. When the very
foundation of the realm is at stake, stern, selfless devotion to duty is the noblest virtue. The welfare of the
kingdom is my only interest."

The chief minister turned to Las Bombas. "Let me
speak with utter honesty. It is no secret that King Augustine is gravely ill. He has not ceased to mourn his
daughter, to such a point that he is no longer capable
of ruling.

"However, I am given to believe that you are a man
of certain talents. I ask you to put them at the service
of your monarch."

"My dear sir," cried Las Bombas, "I consider it an
honor. Had I known this was what you wanted, I
would have presented myself willingly. Now, sir, only
tell me what is required. Do you wish me to treat His
Majesty with Dr. Absalom's Elixir? It has worked
wonders for man and beast and will do no less for a
king. Also, I have in my possession a remarkable stone
from Kazanastan. Or, if you prefer, a vat of magnetized water."

"Trash," said Cabbarus.

"I beg your pardon?"

"Trash," Cabbarus repeated. "You are a common
fraud, a despicable cheat and swindler."

"Yes, and a better man than you," cried Theo, before Musket, reddening, could come to his master's de-
fense. "You talk about virtue and duty. You've turned
them into lies."

"My boy, I beg you! Hold your tongue," the count
pleaded. "Let him call me what he will. If he wants
something I can provide and we can save our necks
with it, let's hear what he has to say."

Mickle, Theo abruptly realized, was no longer at his
side. Cabbarus, ignoring Theo's words, looked past
him toward a corner of the chamber. "Fetch the girl."

The chief minister's voice had an edge of alarm. "Keep her away from there."

The girl was staring down at a wooden trapdoor set in the stone flooring. She did not turn when Theo reached her. She stood frozen, her eyes glazed. Musket had followed Theo and between them they drew her back from the sloping edge.

"It stinks of blood," she murmured. "He's killed people here. I know it."

Mickle's brow was burning to the touch. Theo turned to Cabbarus. "The girl is sick. She must have a doctor. Take her out of this place."

"I doubt that her complaint is serious," replied Cabbarus. "She will recover. In fact, she must."

"Whatever you require of me," put in Las Bombas, "she has no part in it. I urge you to release her. My cures and treatments—she has nothing to do with any of that."

"She has everything to do with it," said Cabbarus. "The king wishes to communicate with the spirit of his daughter. And so he will. There have been reports from a town called Felden. You are known to have summoned ghosts and apparitions with the girl's assistance."

"Do you believe that?" cried Las Bombas, turning pale. "My dear sir, you must understand—and I ask you to keep this a matter of confidence between us— these apparitions, spirit-raisings and all such are, shall we say—"

"False," said Cabbarus. "No more than a mountebank's trickery."

"Exactly!" returned the count, with a certain tone of pride. "Mere illusions, theatrical entertainments. For a moment, I thought you took them as genuine. If His Majesty wishes to reach the spirit of the late princess, the girl can't help him. She can't summon a ghost of any sort, let alone Princess Augusta."

"She will not summon the spirit of the princess," said Cabbarus. "She herself will be the spirit of Augusta. The resemblance between them is striking. She is the age the princess would now have been."

"Impossible!" protested Las Bombas. "She's a street girl. There's no way she can make the king believe she's his daughter."

"How convincing her performance will be," said Cabbarus, "is entirely up to her. For her sake, and yours, I hope it will be persuasive. His Majesty has proclaimed a sentence of death for any who fail him. This is the king's command, not mine. I can do nothing to change it.

"His Majesty knows of your presence. He will grant you a special audience tonight. You will not disappoint him."

"There's no time," said Las Bombas, beginning to sweat. "There are special arrangements to be made. It can't be done."

"You shall have whatever you need," said Cabbarus. "The girl will have only one task. As princess, she will convey a message to her father."

"Message? She can't know what to say to the king."

"She will say what I instruct her to say," replied Cabbarus. "The message is simple, but she must give it precisely. Young woman, I advise you to listen carefully.

"You are to tell His Majesty that your unhappy shade will never rest unless he does what you entreat him. For the sake of his love for you, for his own peace of mind, and for the good of the kingdom, he will give up his throne."

"What?" cried Las Bombas. "Ask the king to abdicate? Leave the throne because—because a ghost wants him to? He'll never do it."

"He will do as his daughter prays him to," said Cabbarus. "As he has always done. In her life, he refused her nothing. He will not refuse her now. Indeed, more than ever, he will grant whatever she desires. I know His Majesty's mind and can assure you of that.

"But there is one thing more. The princess will not only plead for the king to abdicate. She will also urge His Majesty to name a successor. She will tell him that he is to resign his throne in favor of his chief minister."

"You're mad!" cried Theo. "You dare make yourself king!"

"Not I," said Cabbarus. "Princess Augusta shall do it for me. I had once contemplated His Majesty naming me adoptive heir. This is much simpler and saves tiresome waiting. It is only a formality. I rule in fact. I intend to do so in name, as well: Cabbarus the First."

The chief minister stood. "I go to advise His Majesty that I have spoken with you and am convinced your powers are genuine. Meanwhile, you shall make certain the girl understands what she must do. When I return, you shall specify the preparations you desire. If you need a further spur to your efforts, I can tell you that His Majesty offers quite a substantial reward for success. If avoiding death is not sufficient incentive, I am certain that money will be."

Cabbarus strode from the chamber. Las Bombas clapped his hands to his head.

"We're cooked! We'll never pull it off. Oh, my boy, I wish you'd never thought of The Oracle Priestess in the first place. Mickle's a wonder, I know that. But—as Princess Augusta? She'll never manage."

"Do you want her to?" Theo demanded. "King Augustine or King Cabbarus? Florian said there was no difference. I think he was wrong. I don't know whether he's right about the monarchy, or whether

Dr. Torrens is. All I know is that I won't have any part in setting that murderer on the throne."

"The idea of King Cabbarus is distressing, I admit," said the count. "Being dead, even more so. We've got to try it. No, by heaven, we'll do better than try. We'll give him a princess that Augustine can't help but believe. Once the money's in hand, let Cabbarus rule as he pleases. For us, out of the country and on to Trebizonial Mickle, my dear, listen to me—"

"Don't be a fool," cried Theo. "Do you think any of us will get out of this no matter what we do? Do you think Cabbarus will let us live a moment longer than he has to? Knowing what we know? That he set himself up as king on the word of a sham princess? That the whole business was nothing but a trick? He won't dare keep us alive."

The count choked off his words. His face fell. "I hadn't looked at it that way. I'm afraid you have a rather strong point."

Musket, during this, had been examining the trapdoor. Shaking his head in discouragement, he came to rejoin them.

"I thought we could try climbing down that drain or whatever it is. But there's water at the bottom. How deep or where it goes I don't know, and I'm not sure we'd last long enough to find out. Even so, we might risk it."

"Before plunging into some bottomless pit," said Las Bombas, "I'd rather explore another possibility. Let Cabbarus think we'll go along with his scheme. Once we're before the king, we confess the whole business. Throw ourselves on his mercy. Let him know his own chief minister forced us into it."

"Will Augustine believe it?" said Theo. "It's our word against Cabbarus."

Las Bombas nodded ruefully. "I'm afraid you're right. I don't see us winning that argument. It's the end of us, no matter what. We have everything to lose and absolutely nothing to gain. At this point, the only question is our choice of demise: wet or dry?"

24

In Freyborg, what seemed years ago, Justin had said
he would give up his life if Florian asked him. The
idea had seemed heroic and admirable to Theo at the
time. Now he was furious. Dying for Florian was one
thing; dying for the benefit of the chief minister made
him feel soiled. He thought, for a moment, of simply
throwing himself at the throat of Cabbarus and satis-
fying at least some of his rage before the guards killed
him. That would be no help to Mickle, or Musket, or
Las Bombas, who was bemoaning deprivation of life
and fortune both in the same day.

"Chance it, that's what I say," declared Musket.
"Feet first down the shaft, take a breath, and hope for
the best."

"All very well for you," said Las Bombas, who had
gone to see the trapdoor himself. "I'm not the size for
it. I'd end up like a cork in a bottle."

Mickle crouched in a corner, arms clasped around
her shoulders. She stared at the open drain as if unable to turn away.

"Not there," she whispered. Her voice was thin, a
frightened child's.

Theo went to kneel beside her. He glanced at the count. "She's not fit to try anything. I'm not sure she's even able to walk."

Las Bombas glumly nodded. "I feel much the same. Poor girl, if anyone could outface Cabbarus I'd have thought she'd be the one. She's been scared out of her wits from the moment she set foot in here. I don't blame her." The count brightened for a moment. "That might be a blessing in disguise. What if she took sick, eh? Performance canceled due to serious indisposition."

"You won't get away with it," said Musket. "That fish-eyed scoundrel doesn't look the sort to hear excuses. She can't be sick forever. He'll wait. The girl's the one he wants; and suppose in the meantime he decides he doesn't need the rest of us? If we're going to try our luck, it's now or never."

"There's one thing we can do," said Theo, after a time. He hurried on as the idea took better shape in his mind. "Go along with Cabbarus."

"What?" cried Las Bombas. "After all you said against it?"

"Hear the rest," said Theo. "If the king doesn't believe she's his daughter, we're lost from the start. But—suppose Mickle can really make him think she's Princess Augusta? It's doubtful, but she just might be able to do it. If the king listens to her and believes what she says, we may have a chance."

"I don't see that," said the count. "How's it going to help us?"

"Cabbarus wants her to tell the king to give up his throne. What if she does the opposite?"

"Eh? Opposite of what?"

"She tells him to keep it. She tells him never to abdicate, no matter what his chief minister advises. She warns him against Cabbarus, begs the king to dismiss him—"

"And Cabbarus denounces us as frauds."

"Let him," said Theo. "Even if he does, he'll still have a lot to account for."

"It comes to the same," said Las Bombas. "The king may believe us, or he may not. It doesn't answer the question uppermost in my mind: What becomes of us later? Master Cabbarus, I suspect, has a long arm. And the state Mickle's in— Even so, anything's better than jumping into drain pipes."

"Will you try it?" Theo turned to Mickle. On her face was a look of terror he had never seen before. She finally nodded. He smiled at her and would have taken her hand, but she drew away from him.

He had expected Cabbarus. Instead, it was Pankratz who came to order Las Bombas to make his preparations. Theo was unwilling to leave Mickle alone. The count assured him he and Musket could do all that was needed.

Mickle still crouched motionless. Once, she cried out as if in a waking nightmare. The rest of the time, she kept silent. He wondered if she understood or remembered anything of what she must do. He began to despair of his plan. He had thought of no other when the door was unlocked and Las Bombas hurried in.

The count helped Mickle put on a white robe, meantime whispering to Theo, "Musket's waiting. We have it all ready. The draperies, the lights—marvelous, the best I've ever done. It could work. Mickle might well save all our skins."

They were escorted from the chamber, across the courtyard, and entered what Las Bombas told Theo was the New Juliana. Cabbarus awaited them in a large audience hall.

"His Majesty never leaves his apartments," said Cabbarus. "On this occasion, he was consented to do so. I have promised him an event of utmost impor-

tance. Queen Caroline will attend, as well, along with
His Majesty's high councillors and ministers. It is essential for all to hear for themselves what the princess
will instruct her father."

"It's better than what we had in Felden," said Las
Bombas, leading Theo and Mickle behind the curtains
screening a low platform. "One thing I'll say for Cabbarus, he gave me all I wanted. He found some excellent tripods and braziers. I've worked it out so they'll
give off quite impressive smoke. I could have had
fireworks and rockets, but they seemed a touch exces-
sive."

Las Bombas helped Mickle to a tall chair, where
she sat with her head bowed. From the murmur of
voices beyond the curtains, Theo guessed the courtiers
were arriving. The count went to the front of the platform. Mickle's breathing had turned shallow. She did
not answer when Theo spoke to her and gave no sign
she heard him.

Las Bombas ducked around the curtains. "The king
and queen are here. Cabbarus wants us to begin."

"We can't. Not now. Mickle's taken a turn for the
worse. Tell Cabbarus there's been a delay. Tell him—
tell him anything."

"Too late," groaned the count. Musket had lit the
tripods. Clouds of smoke billowed upward. Mickle
raised her head. The girl seemed to be forcing herself
past the limits of her strength.

Theo pulled on the cords that opened the curtains.
In the hall, the candles had been snuffed out. He saw
only a crowd of shadows, two dim figures on a dais at
the far end of the room, and the dark shape of Cabbarus beside them.

The count had arranged lanterns on either side of
Mickle, and their glow fell on her face. The courtiers
drew in their breath at their first sight of the girl. Her
eyes were lowered, her features a pale mask. Her lips

parted slightly but did not move. She spoke in a tone
that seemed to come from a great distance.

"Help me. Please help me. I'm going to fall."

The terror and pleading that underlay the words
were so real that Theo started forward.

"Please," Mickle went on, "give me your hand."

"What's she doing?" Las Bombas whispered franti-
cally to Theo. "She's not supposed to go at it like that.
She's ruining the whole business. If we ever had a
chance, it's gone!"

Mickle had risen from her chair. "Hurry. I can't
hold on any longer."

A cry of anguish rang through the chamber, not
from the king, but from Queen Caroline.

"That is my child! My child is calling!"

25

Theo's head whirled. He had staked all on Mickle's acting her part well; but to mimic a voice she had never heard, the voice of a child long dead, was impossible.

Mickle's tone changed and deepened. It was a new voice, cruel and mocking.

"You seem, Princess, to have put yourself in a fine fix. Let that be a lesson not to pry into places that don't concern you."

The child's voice spoke again. "I was playing hide-and-seek. It was only a game. Please, I'm getting tired."

Mickle had begun making her way like a sleepwalker to the middle of the hall. Theo and Las Bombas were too dumbstruck to prevent her. She spoke once more.

"You take a different air with me now, Princess. I was never one of your favorites. How quickly you change your manner, with your life in my hands. Do you beg me to help you? I am not sure I wish to oblige."

The courtiers gasped. They had realized the same

thing Theo had in the same instant. The voice was a girl's imitating a man; but in tone and cadence, unmistakable: the voice of Cabbarus.

Before Mickle could go on, the chief minister burst out, "What is this monstrous trickery? Majesty, they have deceived me with their promises. They are frauds—"

"Be silent!" cried Augustine. "The spirit of my child at last speaks to me. She tells me truly how she came to her death!"

A dry laugh rose from Mickle's lips. "Many before you, little Princess, made their last journey down this well. Would you find it amusing to join them?"

For all its terror, the child's voice took on a tone of command. "Lift me out. My father shall know how you treated me. He won't like to hear how you stood up there and made fun of me. Some of the ministers want him to send you away. I heard them talking about it. My father hasn't made up his mind. But he will, once he finds out you wouldn't help me."

"He will only know if you live to tell him."

Mickle's eyes were wide, staring upward as she cried out, "My hands are slipping! Cabbarus, don't! You're hurting my fingers!"

Someone was calling for lights. Theo sprang from behind the curtains. Mickle screamed and dropped to the floor. King Augustine was on his feet.

"My daughter did not die by mishap! It was you, Cabbarus! You told me you came too late to save her life. A lie! You were there with her in the Old Juliana. You let her fall to her death. Her spirit accuses you!"

Queen Caroline had reached Mickle. She flung herself beside the unconscious girl. "No spirit! This is my child!"

"Murderer!" cried Augustine. He took a step toward Cabbarus. "Murderer! Seize him!"

Cabbarus leaped away. The guards were as stunned

as the courtiers. He forced his way through the ranks of attendants and fled the chamber. Leaving Mickle and the queen, Theo bolted after him. Cabbarus had gained the corridor and was making for the courtyard.

Theo at his heels, Cabbarus halted, uncertain which way to turn. A company of soldiers had come into sight from one of the arcades. Finding this path of escape blocked, Cabbarus darted through the gate of the Old Juliana. He broke his stride to turn and strike at Theo, who fell to one knee and clutched at the man's robe.

Cabbarus tore free. Guards from the audience chamber were in the courtyard, the alarm raised throughout the palace. Theo grappled with Cabbarus, who threw him aside and clambered up a flight of stone steps.

Theo stumbled after him. The steps narrowed and twisted. It was the belfry of the old fortress. A square gallery with a low railing surrounded the massive bells. Stone arches, open to sky and wind, gave him a dizzying glimpse of the courtyard below.

Cabbarus halted and spun around. Theo heard the growling of an enraged animal. To his horror, he realized it came from his own throat.

He flung himself on the chief minister. Cabbarus fought to break loose. His fingers locked around Theo's neck. Theo pitched backward. Still in the grip of Cabbarus, he lurched against the railing and hurtled over it. He fell, clutching at air for an instant. His hand caught one of the bell ropes.

Cabbarus, toppling with him, loosened his grasp. The man screamed and would have plummeted to the bottom of the tower if Theo had not snatched his arm and held on to it with all his strength.

The jolt nearly wrenched Theo's own arm from its socket. He cried out in pain. The man's weight was dragging at him. Another moment, he feared, and both would fall to their death. He needed only to open his hand to rid himself of his burden.

Cabbarus was staring up at him, eyes bursting with hatred. Theo's own fury choked him. That instant, he wanted nothing so much as to fling the man away. Half sobbing, he clamped his legs around the rope and tightened his grip on Cabbarus.

The guards were racing up the steps into the belfry, with Musket scuttling ahead of them. The dwarf's mouth was open, shouting. Theo heard none of his words. Above him, the bell had stirred into life, its voice resounding in the others that hung beside it. The clangor exploded in his ears. He was being hoisted up and pulled back over the railing, still gripping Cabbarus. Theo's hand had frozen on the man's arm. Someone was prying his fingers loose.

The face of Las Bombas loomed in front of him. Deafened, dazed, he wondered why Mickle had not come. Then he remembered there was no such person. There was only one who had called herself by that name.

26

"They keep telling me I'm Princess Augusta," said Mickle. "I know that. What I can't decide is whether I'm a princess who used to be a street girl, or a street girl who used to be a princess."

Mickle sat cross-legged amid a pile of cushions on her bed in the Royal Chambers. She wriggled her shoulders as if her silken gown made her itch. She grinned at Theo, who waited for her to continue her story. He had not been allowed to see her for two days, while physicians, maids, nurses, and her parents constantly hurried in and out. Finally, Mickle had declared herself perfectly well and demanded Theo, Las Bombas, and Musket.

Queen Caroline sat in a chair by the casement, keeping an anxious eye on her daughter, although the girl had clearly regained health and spirit.

"I remember everything," said Mickle. "That's what makes it feel so odd. Because I can't understand why there were so many years when I'd forgotten everything."

"You didn't forget," said Theo. "It was there, somewhere in your mind. It was in your nightmares."

"They're gone now," said Mickle. "I haven't had any more. Yes, I must have been dreaming about what Cabbarus did to me, but there wasn't any way I could know that. When I saw the trapdoor again, it all started coming back."

"You were living through it again," said Theo. "It was worse than a nightmare because you couldn't wake up from it."

"You gave an impressive performance," put in Las Bombas. "I thought at the time: amazing how you could pretend to be Princess Augusta."

"She wasn't pretending," said Theo. "She was telling us how Cabbarus tried to kill her."

"I suppose it was my own fault," said Mickle. "I was always getting into one scrape or another. I even climbed the bell tower. That day, I wanted to see what was under the trapdoor. I thought it would be a good place for hide-and-seek. Nobody would ever look for me there. But I slipped and couldn't pull myself back. That's when Cabbarus came in and saw me.

"He kicked my hands until I let go. I remember falling down, down into the water. Then there was the river taking me away—"

Queen Caroline came to smooth her daughter's hair. "Do not think of it any longer. We believed you dead. You are alive and with us again. No more need be said."

"Oh, it wasn't too bad after that," Mickle answered. "I was lucky. I floated into the marshes. The Fingers, they're called. The old man who fished me out really saved my life. There's no way I can thank him now. I grew up thinking he was my grandfather. By then, I'd lost my memory of whatever happened before. I couldn't have told him who I was. I didn't know. It was as if I'd always been there. Poor man, he couldn't have heard me, or spoken to me anyway. Even after he taught me his sign language, he never told me how he found me. I suppose he wanted me to stay. And I did, until he died. Then I went off on my own.

"I'll tell you one thing," she added to Queen Caroline. "That Home for Repentant Girls: Something has to be done about it, starting with that oatmeal they serve."

"You shall see to it yourself, my dear," said the queen. "It shall be one of your Royal Duties."

"Oh. Those." Mickle made a face. "I'd rather not think about them."

"Be glad you are able to perform any duties at all," said the queen. "In the audience chamber, we feared you might never wake. You fainted and nothing could bring you back until the bells rang."

"Yes, the bells! How I loved them! Well, Cabbarus tried to kill me—and he turned out to be the one who woke me up. That's fair enough."

"Actually, it was our young friend here," put in Las Bombas. "He was hanging on to the bell rope and Cabbarus at the same time."

"A moment more and the two of them would have ended up with broken necks at the bottom of the tower," added Musket. The dwarf, through methods of his own, had come into possession of a new hat, which he brandished at Theo.

"I kept telling you to let him drop. You didn't hear me. That may be just as well, for some of the names I called you, least of which was 'idiot.'"

"I never hated anyone before," said Theo. "But I hated Cabbarus. Why should I have been the one to save his life?"

"Even so, his life will not be long."

King Augustine had come unannounced into the chamber and had been listening silently. Though he moved with the gait of an invalid still unsure of his legs, his face had regained a little of its color. Although one weight had been lifted from him, he seemed to bear another.

"I blame only myself for raising him to chief minister. It was true, as Princess Augusta told it: I had thought of dismissing him as superintendent of the Royal Household. My senses left me when I believed my child was dead; but I neither excuse nor forgive myself on that account. I will set right all that can be set right. What Cabbarus did in my name can never be forgiven.

"He awaits execution in the Carolia Fortress," the king went on. "He will be put to death justly, as he put to death so many others unjustly. That is the only price he can pay, though it is far too little."

"Majesty, I ask one favor," Theo said. "I didn't save his life to have him lose it. I want no one's death on my conscience, not even his."

"You plead for him?" cried Augustine. "He is a monster!"

"Then let him live with his monstrousness. Banish him—" Theo stopped. "I'm not the one to ask that. Mickle—Princess Augusta—suffered most at his hands. The judgment is hers."

"Well," said Mickle, "I saw what they did to my friend Hanno. I say, no more of it. Yes, send Cabbarus into exile. He's lost his power, and for him that's worse than hanging."

"As you wish," said King Augustine. "He shall know who kept him from the scaffold, and be grateful—if he is capable of gratitude."

"I don't want his gratitude," said Theo. "Majesty, he must not be told I spoke for him."

"So be it," said Augustine. "Councillor Pankratz, too, will be exiled with his master."

"I suggest a desert island," said Las Bombas. "They can take turns ruling each other. But, Your Majesty,

since the matter of granting favors has arisen: I recall
the former chief minister mentioning something about
a reward."

"You're asking for money?" Theo rounded on Las
Bombas. "You want to be paid for something you'd
have done anyway? You ought to be ashamed!"

"I am," replied the count. "On the other hand, I'm
even more ashamed of being penniless."

"A reward was offered," said King Augustine. "You
claim it rightly and shall be given it. But the princess
grows tired. You have our permission to withdraw."

Royal permission being a royal command. Theo,
against his own wishes, found himself ushered from
the chamber with no further chance to talk with Mickle. Or Princess Augusta. How much of her was the
one, how much the other, he was afraid to guess.

"I can't believe you'll take that reward," Theo told
the count as they went to their apartments. "You're a
worse rogue than I thought, if that's possible."

"My boy, what do you expect from me?" protested
Las Bombas. "I'm only flesh and blood—more so than
most."

Theo laughed and shook his head. "I can't argue
that. I'm not the one to blame you, either. I was trying
to be better than I am. I'm not as virtuous as I
thought I was—or wanted to be. I wonder if anyone is,
even Florian. I suppose we should be glad if we're
able to do any good at all."

Las Bombas shrugged. "I never had that kind of
problem."

Las Bombas, despite Theo's reproaches, insisted on
claiming his due. Next day, unable to persuade Theo
to come with him, the count set off with a light heart
and heavy purse. Alone, at loose ends, Theo paced his
chambers. To his surprise, he found himself looking

back with a measure of longing for the days of The
Phrenological Head, even The Oracle Priestess: when
Mickle still was Mickle.

He saw little of her during the following week, the
princess being hedged about with courtiers paying
their respects. The only event to raise his spirits was
the arrival of Dr. Torrens.

News of all that had led to the downfall of Cabbarus had spread throughout the kingdom. The court
physician had set out for Marianstat as soon as word
reached him. Torrens brought the king and queen a
curious gift.

"The river—that is to say, two young water rats—
took me where it had taken the princess, indeed to the
hut itself. At first, I did not realize it. Then I found
this."

Torrens handed Queen Caroline the stained piece of
linen he had worn as a sling. It was a child's garment
embroidered with the Royal Crest, faded and torn but
still visible. "I took it as proof the princess was dead.
Instead, it was a token that she still lived."

King Augustine, over the doctor's protest, named
Torrens chief minister. Augustine then ordered him to
announce pardon to all whom Cabbarus had unjustly
sentenced, as well as those who had attacked the
Nierkeeping garrison. The doctor, describing Florian
to the king, doubted this would satisfy him.

"We spent many days together," said Torrens. "We
did not agree, nor did I expect us to. As a man, I respect him more than I imagined I would. As chief
minister, I am troubled by him. He has not rejoined
his friends in Freyborg. Where he is, I do not know.
But he has not changed his views of the monarchy. I
suspect we shall hear again of Master Florian."

Later, he spoke apart with Theo.

"Their Majesties are concerned for your future and

so am I. Certain matters must be discussed, of importance to you and to the kingdom."

"And Princess Augusta?"

"Naturally. We shall speak of this another time. Meanwhile, I have something Florian wished me to give you. It amused him that you, of all people, were the one to bring down Cabbarus. I think he was a little envious, too. He had counted on doing that himself. He would, no doubt, have gone about it differently. The fact remains: Cabbarus is gone."

"Was I a fool?" asked Theo. "Should I have let him drop? I didn't want his death on my conscience, but I don't want his life on my conscience, either."

"I do not know what I would have done in the same circumstances," replied Torrens. "How easy it is to think well of ourselves. Until the moment is upon us, we can never be certain."

Torrens handed Theo a folded scrap of paper.

"From Florian. He asks you to remember some things you said to him at the farm. It would appear you gave him much to think about."

Afterwards, in his chambers, Theo smiled over the hastily written lines:

My Child,
You did well. Perhaps you even did right.

It was unsigned.

27

Torrens finally did what Mickle had not managed to do. As physician as well as chief minister, he ended the endless visitations by the courtiers. Instead, he prescribed fresh air. Theo was permitted to walk with her in the Juliana gardens, leaving her ladies-in-waiting behind them to cluck over such a breach of etiquette. For a while, the two were silent, content simply to be in each other's company.

"There's quite a difference between all this and the way I lived in Freyborg," Theo said at last. "Jellinek's tavern, the wine merchant's cellar. Stock and the others. I miss them. I even miss my cubbyhole on Strawmarket Street. But I realize I'd have been a fool to bring a princess there."

"I didn't know I was a princess, so it wouldn't have mattered."

"But you are a princess, and it matters now. There's no way around it."

"I'm still Mickle, aren't I? One part of me."

"The king and queen don't think so. I have an idea they wish you'd forget that part."

"Not likely!" Mickle suddenly imitated the voice of a street peddler and laughed at the startled look on Theo's face. "They've been talking to you, haven't they? Yes, well, they've been talking to me, too. They mainly come back to the same thing: I'll be queen of Westmark some day."

"And so you will."

"Not if Florian has his way. Not if I have mine, either. There must be a royal cousin somewhere who's foolish enough to like this kind of work. Anyhow, I told them I didn't care about it, I wouldn't let them separate us. So that settles it." When Theo did not answer immediately, her face fell. "Doesn't it? Unless—What did they say to you?"

"Only that I had to make my own choice."

A flurry of excitement from the court ladies interrupted him.

Theo turned to see Las Bombas hurrying up the path, and called out to him. "You, back again? I thought you'd be well away by now, money and all."

"No," said Las Bombas. "That's why I'm here."

"You changed your mind about keeping it!" exclaimed Theo. "I never imagined you would. Bravo, then!"

"I admit having such a large sum made me feel uncomfortable. I'm more used to pursuing a fortune than having one handed to me."

"So you had to return it." Theo clapped Las Bombas on the shoulder. "You do have some sort of conscience after all."

"Yes, and it's been a torment to me." The count sighed. "I can't forgive myself."

"Of course you can," said Theo. "You'll feel better as soon as you turn back the reward."

"You misunderstand," said Las Bombas. "I can't forgive myself—for losing it.

"Bilked out of it," he went on ruefully. "Gulled out

of it, as if I'd been an innocent babe. That's what's unforgivable. I fell in with a gentleman—Gentleman? A barefaced scoundrel! He showed me a letter from a nobleman who'd been clapped into a Trebizonian prison. If we'd pay his ransom and get him out, he'd show us where he'd discovered an enormous buried treasure. We'd go shares—ah, no need to parade the details of my shame before the world. The money's gone. Oh, let me come across that wretch again!

"So I've only stopped to bid you farewell once more, Princess. And you, my boy. Musket's impatient to be off. You two, I daresay, are busy making your own plans."

"I have none," said Theo. "But Dr. Torrens has one for me. I don't know. I was telling Mickle—the princess—I'll have to decide. Dr. Torrens wants me to travel around Westmark."

"You'll do it in fine style," said Las Bombas. "Rather better than we did."

"No. Just the opposite. He wants me to be on my own and see for myself what the kingdom's like. He thinks I can find out what the people want and what's to be done about it. But I don't know if I can. I don't even know whether Florian's right, or the monarchy."

"Permit me to say," put in Las Bombas, "no offense, you understand, but a princess who smokes a pipe, swears like a trooper, and scratches wherever she itches might be a blessing for the entire kingdom. Even Florian might approve."

"What if—" Theo took Mickle's hand. "What if you and I went together? You'd know more than I would. I've hardly been away from Dorning."

The girl's eyes were dancing, but she shook her head. "I'll stay here. For now, at any rate. My parents broke their hearts over me once. I won't have them break again. I didn't like it when you walked off last time. I won't mind so much now. It's not the same thing. Do what Dr. Torrens asks. You want to. I know it. I can tell by looking at you."

"I don't want to leave you."

"You won't," said Mickle. "Call it being slightly apart for a while."

The ladies-in-waiting had come to insist on taking the princess indoors. Mickle stuck out her tongue at them, but finally let them escort her to the New Juliana. She turned back once and Theo read the quick motion of her hands.

"Find what you want. I will find you."